'It's refreshi...
sure of her ...

'Too many wome...
about the fact that the only thing they want from a relationship is raw sex. I find it. . .quite electrifyingly exciting that you're prepared to be so honest and I very much look forward to getting our relationship onto that footing as soon as we possibly can.'

Nicole stiffened, suddenly alarmed, and her eyes widened. That wasn't what she'd meant, was it? Did 'no commitment' instantly translate into 'immediate sex and nothing else'?

After living in the USA for nearly eight years, **Lilian Darcy** is back in her native Australia with her American husband and their three young children. More than ever, writing is a treat for her now, looked forward to and luxuriated in like a hot bath after a hard day. She likes to create modern heroes and heroines with good doses of zest and humour in their make-up, and relishes the opportunity that the medical series gives her for dealing with genuine, gripping drama in romance and in daily life. She finds research fascinating too—everything from attacking learned medical tomes to spending a day in a maternity ward.

Recent titles by the same author:

INCURABLY ISABELLE
A SPECIALIST'S OPINION
MISLEADING SYMPTOMS
A GIFT FOR HEALING
FULL RECOVERY

MAKING BABIES

BY
LILIAN DARCY

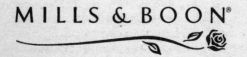

*MILLS & BOON and MILLS & BOON with the Rose Device
are registered trademarks of the publisher.*

*First published in Great Britain 1997
Harlequin Mills & Boon Limited,
Eton House, 18-24 Paradise Road, Richmond, Surrey TW9 1SR*

© Lilian Darcy 1997

ISBN 0 263 80638 3

*Set in Times 10 on 10½ pt. by
Rowland Phototypesetting Limited
Bury St Edmunds, Suffolk*

03-9802-52508-D

*Printed and bound in Great Britain
by Mackays of Chatham PLC, Chatham*

CHAPTER ONE

NEW snow blanketed the city of Columbus, which the winter-weary residents of central Ohio felt was definitely unfair since it was now March—*well* into March, actually—and, as the cold weather had arrived earlier than usual, it could at least have had the grace to depart again with similar promptitude.

There was one person in Columbus who greeted the sight of all that whiteness with pleasure, though. Still somewhat afflicted with jet lag as she had only arrived from Australia late on Friday night, Nicole Martin had to struggle to obey the imperious command of the clock-radio alarm at six-thirty, but once she was up. . .

'Oh, *look*, Astro!' she told Barb Zelinsky's cat, leaning on the window-sill and looking out into Barb's still, silent garden. 'Just *look*! It's even on the telephone wires and dusting that little conifer, like a Christmas tree! It's falling like someone shaking a feather bed!'

Astro—short, Barb had said, for Cat Astrophe— remained unimpressed. He had seen it before.

Nicole hadn't. She was from Sydney, where even a light frost was a newsworthy event, and her relationship with snow had been thus far limited to one spring weekend some years ago at Smiggin Holes in the Snowy Mountains, where she and her friends had thrown snowballs and careened down slushy, half-bare slopes in makeshift sleds, shrieking a lot and getting very wet. She had loved that, too, but *this*. . .! Just beautiful!

There was no opportunity for further contemplation, however, as she was starting work this morning and hadn't allocated any time in her morning schedule for

5

the rapt admiration of snow. She had to shower, dress, eat breakfast, feed Astro *and*, she suddenly realised, clean all that lovely feathery white stuff off Barb's car, then drive it on the no doubt glacially slippery roads across the river to Riverbank Hospital.

All at once it was a little daunting.

She and Barbara Zelinsky had, in essence, swapped lives for a year as part of a nursing exchange programme so, while Nicole was here living in Barb's very nice three-bedroomed house in the neighbourhood of Northmoor—just across the river from the hospital— Barb would be ensconced in Nicole's much smaller flat in the Sydney suburb of Randwick. Barb hadn't minded about the disparity in size of dwelling.

'Your balcony, and all that sunshine!' she'd told Nicole during their two-day overlap in Sydney. 'The beaches! I won't be spending any time indoors at all.'

She had been enthusiastic about the job, too, as a practice nurse for an obstetrician in solo practice with visiting rights at Royal Prince Alfred Hospital.

'He seems quite a specimen,' she had said of Dr Gary Hill. 'Is he. . .um. . .married?'

'Divorced,' Nicole had answered, and Barb's dark eyes had glinted significantly.

In her early forties, she was divorced herself, apparently. 'Sure I want to marry again!' she had said in response to Nicole's tentative question. 'That's half the reason I wanted this exchange. A chance to meet new people.'

Nicole wanted to meet new people, too, but definitely *not* in order to marry one of them. 'Me, I'm out for a good time,' she'd told Barb very firmly.

'Well, why not, you're only. . .what?'

'Twenty-six.'

'Then, yes, you'd be crazy to settle down if you don't feel ready!'

There was quite a bit more to it than that, as it happened, but in two days Nicole hadn't become quite intimate enough with Barbara to go into her deeper reasons for avoiding commitment.

Helping Barb to settle in had taken up most of their time, and then had come the day of Nicole's own departure. Armed with volumes of information about Astro's personal foibles and how to understand the channels on the cable TV, Nicole only realised during the long flight that she hadn't learned much about the practice in which she'd be working. She knew the basic facts. It was a large Ob/Gyn practice with five partners, who had offices adjacent to Riverbank Hospital. Nicole would be working mainly for the senior obstetrician in the practice, Dr Richard Gilbert.

If this house had been taller and the surrounding trees smaller, she might have been able to see the cluster of modern hospital buildings from here but, with the river to cross as well as a large highway, there was little temptation to walk—which brought her back to her morning schedule and the fact that it was now very tight.

Perhaps she shouldn't have insisted quite so adamantly to Darla Hogan yesterday that she'd be able to manage on her own today and didn't need a ride. Darla, who was one of the seven other nurses in the practice, had met Nicole's plane on Friday night, brought her here to the house and helped her settle in.

She had come by the place earlier in the day to turn up the heat and stock the fridge with basics, and then on Saturday she'd had Nicole over for an evening meal with her husband and family of three teenage children, who had been a lot of fun. On Sunday, Darla had had other commitments but she had phoned to check how things were going, which was the point at which Nicole had perhaps been a little too breezily confident in her ability to manage.

Trying not to be too intimidated—the snow was still falling, more thickly than ever now, although in another part of the sky the clouds seemed to be breaking up—Nicole raced through the other tasks of the morning, then put her new dark plum-coloured coat over her white uniform, jammed her new plum-coloured wool cloche hat over her extravagant and disobedient carroty-red hair to create a pleasing clash of colour, donned her new black leather gloves and marched out to the car.

Gee, the stuff was inches thick! Feathery light, though. Could you just drive through it? Did it slip like ice, or ball up stickily on the wheels like mud? No, surely this powder was far too dry and ephemeral for that!

She lifted her face into it—the air was so cold it tingled—closed her eyes to let the flakes catch in her lashes and felt the crystal brightness of sunshine against her closed lids. Those clouds were definitely lifting, parting and shredding even as she stood here. She opened her eyes again, and this time it was like utter magic.

The snow was still falling and yet the early sun shone so that she was being showered in a fall of light, brilliant diamonds. She laughed aloud, forgetting about getting to work, scooped up handfuls of the snow and threw them into the air to add even more sparks of white crystal. She impulsively took off her hat and shook out her hair, still laughing as the snow settled on her bare, bright head.

And that was how Richard Gilbert first saw her.

He'd been driving very slowly on the slippery roads. The quiet streets of Northmoor didn't rate a very high priority when it came to ploughing and salting, and there hadn't yet been enough traffic to render this pristine stuff into dirt-grey slush, so his car slid almost silently to a halt at the kerb just in front of Barb's house.

This girl—Nicole Martin—hadn't heard his approach, or had assumed it was a neighbour. Or perhaps she was just so absorbed in that magic, sparkling world she was creating around herself that she'd simply tuned everything else out. Whatever. . .it didn't matter. What mattered was that he had climbed out of the car and reached the driveway where she stood, still unaware of him, which gave him plenty of time to look at her and conclude with an initial blank amazement that she looked incredibly like Linda!

He stood, as transfixed as she was, and tallied the similarities. . .and the differences. The same hair. It was what they called strawberry blonde, he thought, but that didn't do justice to this brilliant shade of pink gold at all. Whereas Linda's had been tinted, permed and cropped into a sophisticated little bob, though, Nicole Martin's streamed and rioted halfway down her back and fell around her high forehead in soft yet intricate curls, like a pre-Raphaelite painting, and he suspected that no hairdresser had been near it for a good year or more.

The same figure, too, although, as Nicole lifted her hands to scoop more of that feathery snow into the air, he decided she was even taller than Linda's five feet nine inches and athletically graceful rather than poised like a model, as Linda was. The same skin, except that Linda was his own age, thirty-six now, and when he had last seen her a year ago she was starting to achieve that peachy perfection through make-up rather than nature. Ms Martin was clearly some years younger.

And yet—he stepped closer—her face was not entirely without lines, faint ones etched parallel across her brow and some even fainter ones around her mouth, which suggested that at one time she had held those pretty bow-shaped lips in a tight tuck under the influence of pain. This observation gave him to wonder a little.

Then suddenly a darker emotion entered the picture, and he experienced a hot spurt of irritation even as there came an unwilling tightening in his loins.

I don't need this, he thought angrily. I really don't. What a maddening coincidence. What *is* it about red-headed women?

But he was so close now that he had to speak. 'Excuse me. . .' he began on a growl.

'Oh!' Nicole gave a squeaky yelp of surprise but recovered herself enough to say, 'Um. . . Hi!' Then she instinctively stepped back a pace.

The natives in these parts were probably friendly but this one certainly didn't look it, and he'd given her a start, too, with that gruff, abrupt phrase. Nicole felt more than a little foolish at having been discovered showering herself in snow, and from his expression he wasn't impressed at her behaviour either.

How long had he been watching her? He was looking at her as if he knew her and didn't like her and, no matter how quickly she piled on the first impressions now, she sensed that he was way ahead of her.

She tallied those impressions quickly. Dark hair, very dark eyes, dressed in a black padded coat, taller than her own five feet ten but not so tall that he was massive or towering. He looked intelligent and seasoned enough in years to be interesting, and he looked as if he had definitely got out of the wrong side of whatever opulent and masculine bed he'd slept in—which was quite enough to decide about a man after not more than four seconds of scrutiny.

'Can I—?' she began.

'I'm Richard Gilbert,' he interrupted in a dark voice that had a little scrape of huskiness in it and an accent that was American, of course—attractively so, she might have considered, if it hadn't sounded so irritable.

'You're going to be my nurse. I expect Barb gave you a run-down—you *are* Nicole Martin, aren't you?' he appended impatiently.

'Yes.' She nodded quickly, realising that her blank look was understandably throwing him off. And she saw now that he was wearing royal blue hospital scrubs beneath that black coat. 'Yes, of course I am. Sorry, I'm just feeling. . .silly for letting you sneak up on me while I was going ga-ga over the snow.'

But if she'd expected her honesty to undercut that aura of faint hostility. . .

'Did I sneak?' he wanted to know.

A petty quibble, she considered, but conceded, 'I suppose it's difficult to be noisy in snow. It was my fault. I was in a daze. Can we call it jet lag?' she begged sweetly.

'Let's not,' he suggested on a drawl, and if that odd hostility still simmered beneath the surface it was well masked now. 'That's not nearly a good enough title for the picture I saw.' He smiled, a complex action in that intelligent face. It narrowed the corners of those *very* dark eyes and twisted his firm-lipped mouth a little. 'How about "Maiden Blessing the Snow"?'

'Oh.' She laughed, then blushed and felt, for a moment, quite flustered under his dark gaze. 'Don't tease! I marched out here all ready to do battle with the stuff on my car—Barb's car—and then it was so beautiful I just forgot—about *everything*.' Clapping her hands to her cheeks, she suddenly said in a horrified voice, 'You've come to get me because I'm late, haven't you? No wonder you were—'

'*Relax*! You're not late, although. . .' he glanced at his watch. . .'we should get going or we both will be. I came by because I suspected you hadn't encountered snowy roads before.'

'And you were right!'

'And I thought it might be safer and less nerve-wracking for you if I gave you a lift in.'

'Thanks. That was nice of you,' she told him soberly, 'to go out of your way.'

'It wasn't out of my way. I only live a few streets from here.' He gestured, not a very clear movement but she noticed his hands and how well formed they were, with smooth skin, squarish pink nails and just a sprinkling of dark hair on their backs. She noticed, too, that the hostility was back in his tone and manner. 'You'll see my place,' he went on, 'because I'd better have you to dinner as soon as I can.'

'Oh, don't put yourself out,' she returned with a definite bite.

'I won't,' he answered absently as they walked to his car. 'I'm not much of a cook.'

'Then why have me at all?'

'Because you don't know anyone here, and I promised Barb.'

'Well, Dr Gilbert, I'd be happy to release you from that promise, on Barb's behalf,' she assured him with dry cheek. 'I'm a fairly capable person, actually, and can probably carry on with my existence here without the benefit of dinner at your place.'

'I'll take you out, if you'd like that better.'

She still got the sense that his mind was elsewhere and felt her own anger mounting. On the one hand, he'd been very considerate, coming to get her in the snow. On the other, he was acting as if she was a bratty child he'd been forced to babysit against his will.

With an obstinate need to goad him now, she said calmly, 'Yes, much better. I want Columbus's best restaurant, please. Don't think you can fob me off with bad home cooking!'

They had reached the car and his head shot up to study her, his hand arrested in the act of putting his key in the door. He looked astounded, too astounded to have yet decided if he was furious. Realising that her boats were already well and truly burned, she simply grinned.

'Don't worry. Didn't mean it. You obviously don't want to give me dinner at all so don't, please. I won't hold it against you.'

He had snow on the roof of his car, and after they'd stared at each other for a long, belligerent moment across the crystal white expanse she couldn't help touching it, then watching how those dry feathers melted to nothing on her gloved finger. Fabulous stuff!

She knew he was still studying her but didn't dare to look up any more. Her momentary boldness was disappearing as quickly as those crystals she held. Her heart was racing and she thought, I might have made him really angry. I shouldn't have called his bluff. I've got to work with him every day for a year! Barb should have warned me that he was—

'Tired. I'm sorry,' he said at last. 'I delivered nine babies on the weekend. I only went home for breakfast.'

'That's fine. I understand,' she told him quickly. 'Nine! Wow!'

'I was covering for the whole practice.'

It was a perfectly reasonable explanation and Nicole didn't believe a word of it, though she couldn't have said why. There was more to it than mere fatigue. On the surface that impatient irritation seemed to have gone now, but she still felt. . .aware of him somehow, conscious of his complexity and a little disturbed at how much she'd let him see of her own emotions in only a few minutes—her giddy response to the snow, her angry response to him.

'And I'm sorry I had to deputise Darla to meet you and settle you in.' He stifled another yawn. 'Let's go!'

She was seated beside him in the car a moment later. We didn't actually resolve the issue of dinner, she thought. I hope he *doesn't* ask. . .although I know Dr Hill was going to take Barb out. If he does push it I'll have to accept or I'll look rude—*and* insipid. And didn't I say I wanted a good time here?

Richard Gilbert's car was rather low-slung, with a seat that hugged her closely but didn't support her back in quite the right place so that it twinged with sudden pain as he took a corner, and reminded her just why she'd been so keen to arrange this nursing exchange and was now so restlessly determined on a butterfly social life.

The accident. And Colin.

She shuddered at the very thought of it all and felt again the intense desire for freedom she'd known for the past year and a half and an utter panic and reaction at the very idea of any involvement in a serious relationship.

Nicole wanted it 'lite'—frothy and fun and sweet. She wanted to go out on the town with a good-looking, interesting man who would make her laugh, make her feel alive, then drop her home again alone at the end of the evening and *not* expect a detailed accounting of everything she did when they weren't together. Yes, very definitely 'lite', with no calorie-rich commitment dragging her down. She shuddered again and shifted to try and ease the nagging discomfort in her back.

Beside her, as he turned into River Road, Richard was aware of the little movement but interpreted it as a reaction to the cold. Nicole Martin wasn't used to this weather. And that was another thing she shared with Linda, who had always hated the long, dull Columbus winter. Linda lived in Los Angeles now.

How on earth could he have kidded himself for so long that there was any future in their relationship? Why hadn't he set out his terms sooner? It was a pointless regret, however, and one he was determined not to dwell on. Hadn't dwelled on for some time, in fact, only now there was to be this Nicole Martin like a daily thorn in his side with her resemblance to Linda, *reminding* him.

I don't *need* this! he thought again, then decided with the steely determination that was customary to him that he was going to conquer it, and soon. The question was how.

He turned into Alfred Street then took the lane that swung round in front of the entrance to Riverbank's North Tower, evolving strategies all the while.

'This is where I'll have to drop you off,' he told Nicole, pulling up sharply and staring ahead, his train of thought abruptly cut off. She drew in a breath that was a hiss of pain and he turned to her, alarmed. 'Hey!'

'Just my back. Sorry.'

'No, *I'm* sorry. I was. . .thinking, and stopped too suddenly. You've got back trouble?'

'Yes,' Nicole told him. 'I was in a car accident a couple of years ago. Spinal injury, amongst other things. Three months' traction in hospital.'

'Not fun,' he acknowledged briefly.

'Not much,' she drawled. 'It's doing pretty well these days, but I've got to be careful. No heavy lifting or frequent bending, which is why I had to give up midwifery and turn to Ob practice nursing. The flight from Sydney—over twenty-four hours—didn't do it much good, I'm afraid, so it's more iffy than usual. It really wasn't your fault.'

'You're letting me off too easily,' he said with a smile.

'Everyone deserves one chance,' she answered him lightly.

'And that was mine?'

' 'Fraid so,' she said laughingly.

He gave her easy directions to the lift and to Riverbank Ob/Gyn's suite in the North Tower's top floor, then drove off in the direction of the doctors' car park so that she was left on the kerb, struggling a little with the slippery snow but oddly happy now after that awkward start with the man. Well, she reasoned, the snow, the new job, a hundred interesting impressions to absorb and evidently she hadn't entirely sabotaged her future working relationship with the difficult Dr Gilbert. So, yes, she was happy.

Not questioning the mood any more deeply, she skittered across to the North Tower entrance and let the automatic doors usher her inside at precisely ten to eight.

CHAPTER TWO

'THAT was nice of him,' Darla Hogan said when Nicole explained that Dr Gilbert had given her a lift in to work. They were in the nurses' lab, and Darla had started to show her where various supplies were kept.

'Yes, I thought so. Is he always. . .?' She hesitated, on the verge of asking about the man's display of irritation. Is he always that way when he's tired? But at the last moment she changed tack and substituted, 'That thoughtful?'

'Unless he's rushed off his feet—which I was this morning, getting the kids ready for school, or I'd have thought myself that you'd have trouble with the snow.'

'It would have been something of a challenge,' Nicole conceded.

'Tell me, though, did Dr Gilbert *say* anything when he—? That is, did he give the impression of—?' Darla seemed to realise that she wasn't making much sense— Nicole's politely baffled look would have provided a clue as to that—and after a moment's hesitation said bluntly, 'You see, you look so much like Linda.'

'Linda?'

'Obviously he didn't say. Well, he wouldn't, would he? I noticed it the moment I saw you at the airport. The same hair, blue eyes, fair skin, fine features, willowy build. For one awful moment I even thought—but then I realised she couldn't have grown her hair out so much in just over a year.'

'Um. . .'

'His ex-girlfriend,' Darla explained at last.

'Ouch!' Nicole said. 'Perhaps I should dye my hair.'

'Oh, no, I shouldn't think it'll be a problem,' came

17

the reassuring response. 'We all got the impression that it wasn't a very *committed* relationship.' Nicole pricked up her ears. 'They were together for quite a while, but they never lived together. In fact, we sometimes wondered what they *did* do together, other than eating out and one or two other obvious things. And since they broke up he's been out with all sorts of women. We all hope he'll find someone and settle down—'

'Oh, no,' Nicole blurted rashly. 'He sounds like just the kind of man I like! That is,' she added hastily, on seeing Darla's somewhat shocked expression, 'you wouldn't want to work for a man who was suffering from a broken heart, would you?'

'True. . .'

'Um, should I unpack these boxes of pregnancy tests?' Distraction suddenly seemed like a good tactic. She didn't even know herself quite why she'd reacted that way—and aloud, too.

Somehow, though, the idea of 'eating out and one or two other obvious things' sounded like just what she was looking for at the moment. With a man like Richard Gilbert, though? Her spirit rebelled against the idea with surprising force. At first glance, he would seem to fill her stated criteria, and yet there was nothing about him that quite fitted the word 'lite'.

'Yes,' was Darla's answer to her question, 'if the others are all used up. Which, yes, I see they are. And that reminds me, you'll need to stock the warming drawer in the bottom of the examining table in each room with speculums in several different sizes—here they are in the autoclave—and remember to switch the heater on for the warming drawer when you first come in. . .'

So the morning began. Orientation ranged from sketchy to non-existent, and Nicole decided that for Barb's sake it might be better not to mention that they'd spent far more time during their two days together in

Sydney talking about the latter's divorce than about Riverbank Ob/Gyn.

Darla gave her enough of a tour to enable her to navigate her way from front office to chart room to waiting room to lab, and she had time to take in an impression of carefully thought out decor in each partner's office, colourful toys for bored toddlers in the waiting room and a general aura of immaculate cleanliness, detailed professionalism and attractive efficiency throughout, but that was about all.

Everyone clearly assumed that she knew considerably more than she did about the staff and the weekly routine, which made for some potentially awkward moments during the course of the day, but as the work itself was familiar and not hard there was a certain wicked pleasure involved in staying just ahead of minor disaster.

Or, on one occasion, *not* staying ahead of it. And naturally it was Richard Gilbert who was the one to observe her politely ushering a very pregnant patient into a very tiny storage closet instead of the ultrasound room where he was due to check the baby's size in order to assess Mrs Tillich's chances of a vaginal birth after her previous Caesarean.

His smile was dry and so was his tone as he put his hand over the phone and suggested, 'Try two doors along. Those are the clean gowns, and she won't need one today.' Then he went back to the patient on the phone. 'Yes, Mrs Allyson. I think you should definitely come in.'

It seemed auspicious, too, that this first day of hers was to be known for months afterwards as 'the day Lorraine Miller had her baby in the office', although in the end that wasn't the part of it that stuck most strongly in Nicole's mind.

At half past two things in the practice were deceptively normal. Dr Kramer was just finishing a delivery, Dr Mason and Dr Turabian were seeing patients and Dr

Smith had the day off. There were several patients waiting, mostly for Dr Kramer whose schedule had been thrown off by the delivery but it had been a simple one and she was expected back any minute.

Mrs Miller, who was at thirty-eight weeks gestation with her third child, had come in for her weekly check-up and had requested a nurse as chaperon. This was her right, and there was a notice to that effect on the inside of every examining room door, but Nicole suspected that she was there more as a babysitter for two very energetic little girls than because Mrs Miller had any fears about inappropriate behaviour from Dr Gilbert.

The girls, aged four and two, were sweet with their soft, ash-blonde hair and large blue eyes, but they were a handful.

'Why does Mommy have to get undressed? Why does she have a paper sheet on her?'

''Zine! I want to read the 'zine. Mommy, that's *my* 'zine!'

'The doctor has to check the baby, Ashley. Brittany, the nice nurse will read you the magazine. *No*, Ashley, Brittany had it first. The paper sheet is so I don't get cold.'

Dr Gilbert arrived and Nicole did start to read the magazine to the little girls in order to stem the flow of questions and demands, which meant that Mrs Miller eventually had time to say, 'Doctor, you said you'd hurry the baby along a bit this week. . .'

'I did, and I will,' Richard Gilbert answered cheerfully, putting on fresh gloves. He still wore his blue scrubsuit, too, which clung softly to his body, revealing its strength and fluidity of line. He looked very relaxed dressed that way, and very much at home in this domain of his. 'Let's see, a week ago you were nearly five centimetres dilated already, weren't you?'

'Yes, and you said the sonogram showed that the

baby already weighed a good seven pounds.'

'Closer to seven and a half, probably, which means he'd be almost eight by now.'

'You said "he"!' Mrs Miller accused suspiciously, lifting her head to look at the doctor.

'Yes, but I was purely using the generic masculine,' he answered very swiftly and quite calmly, measuring Lorraine Miller's swollen belly.

'Oh. So I might be having a girl. . .'

'Or you might not,' he agreed, smiling crookedly. 'You said you didn't want to know.'

'*You* know, though.'

'I'm afraid so.' He found the foetal heartbeat with ease and they all listened to its strong, rhythmic sound for a moment. 'The. . .er. . .information floated past on the sonogram last week and I couldn't avoid knowing, but you did say—'

'And I meant it, but it's hard when you're teasing me like this.'

'I'm sorry. Can't resist it.' He grinned. 'You'll know soon enough, I think. Let's see what we can do here. . .' He began the internal exam. 'You're a good five centimetres. Closer to six.'

'I've been having episodes of Braxton-Hicks contractions over the past few days. Ouch!'

Nicole went on valiantly 'reading' during all of this, which meant mainly pointing out any interesting pictures she could find, but the girls were prone to distraction. 'Why did you say ouch just now, Mommy?'

'Because it hurts. Um, Dr Gilbert. . .'

'I know.' He nodded. 'Sorry. It's commonly known as stripping your membranes. I'm running my finger around the inside of the half-opened cervix, between it and the baby's head—which is already nicely in place. I'm very good at this,' he announced, cheerfully smug. 'And it almost always works. It releases a hormone which will stimulate labour, and as you're half-dilated and almost fully effaced it should do the trick over the next day or two.'

'In that case, I'll put up with it, then, because it has to be less painful—*ou-ouch*—than pushing out a big baby like Brittany was. This one would be over nine pounds if I had to wait two more weeks, wouldn't it?'

'There's no way you're going two more weeks, Lorraine!' he said firmly. 'There!' He took off his gloves. 'Now, when you go into labour just call the office or the answering service and then come straight in because there won't be any waiting around with this one!'

He left, grinning again, and Nicole gained the impression of a far more attractive bedside manner than she'd have given him credit for this morning during certain moments in their first encounter.

Mrs Miller turned to her as she eased herself clumsily off the table. 'Thanks! My mother couldn't take the girls today, and my husband had a meeting. Do you think he meant what he said about the "generic masculine"?'

'I have no idea,' Nicole answered truthfully, still smiling a little at the memory of his cheerful confidence on the issue. 'I expect he did.'

She was rather curious now herself. These lively girls might do well with a baby brother to torture with some over-enthusiastic affection.

'Doesn't Mommy have funny big underwear?' little Ashley was saying as Mrs Miller turned to her pile of clothing.

Nicole let herself out to give the woman some privacy, observing that she was still in discomfort from what Dr Gilbert had done. A few minutes later, as she was weighing the next patient and testing her urine sample, she heard Mrs Miller say to the girls on their way out, 'Yes, we can play with the toys in the waiting room a bit more. I'd like the chance to sit down for a few minutes, anyway.'

She was still sitting there fifteen minutes later when Nicole came out to call another patient. Two women were booked for appointments every fifteen minutes so turnover was quick. Between the two of them, she and Dr Gilbert had dispatched four more patients since Mrs Miller—three Ob checks and an annual pap—with no unexpected problems cropping up. Now both the three o'clock appointments were here as well. Nicole called the first one back, weighed her and sent her in to produce a urine specimen, then came back to Mrs Miller.

'You don't look very comfortable, Lorraine. . .'

'It's aching all across my lower stomach, and it feels as if the baby's going to just fall out. It's not like labour, though. . .' She stood up, then grimaced. 'Actually, maybe it *is* like labour. . .' And then her waters broke and gushed out in a warm, splashy flood all over the chair and the carpeted floor. 'Oh, my goodness, I'm so sorry. . .*ah-h-h*! OK, this is now *definitely* like labour.'

'It *is* labour,' Nicole said. 'Don't worry about the mess. It's really only water. Now, can we call your husband? Um. . .*Trish*?' She called the trimly uniformed receptionist over.

Meanwhile, the six pregnant ladies also in the waiting room were wildly curious and the two first-time fathers-to-be who had supportively accompanied their wives were struggling not to look appalled. 'Could you walk Lorraine over to Labor and Delivery, Trish?'

'Walk?' Lorraine was doubtful and alarmed.

'The tower is connected to the hospital,' Nicole promised. 'It's carpeted corridor and nice elevators all the way.'

'I don't think there's. . .ah-h-h. . .time,' she said.

'Oh, I'm sure there is,' Nicole started to say. It was understandable that women in labour often thought—or hoped—that they were further along than they really were.

This time, though. . .

'No, there really isn't,' Lorraine said. 'I'm starting to want to—' She stopped abruptly and began to pant for all she was worth.

Somehow the news had reached Richard Gilbert. He appeared very suddenly and said to the waiting room in general, 'Don't worry, everyone. Fourth time this week so we're quite used to it.' Since nobody was quite sure if he was joking they were all suddenly silent. 'Trish,' he went on quickly, 'keep an eye on the girls, and phone. . .?' He raised an enquiring eyebrow at Lorraine.

'555 6213,' she gasped. 'My husband. They'll have to get him out of the meeting.'

'First, though, Trish, get a warming table sent over from Labor and Delivery, *stat*. Nicole?'

They both had to support Mrs Miller as they led her back to the examining room she had so recently left, and she had two contractions on the way, panting desperately through each of them. The third gripped her as soon as she was up on the table, while Nicole was still frantically hunting up scissors for the cord, a suction bulb, towels for the bleeding, a basin for the placenta and some disposable drapes to protect at least partially the carpet and the patient herself.

'OK, head's crowning,' Dr Gilbert said. 'This one's not blonde, Lorraine. . .'

'Can I push now?'

'Yes, give it a try. I don't think you'll have to work too hard. OK, deep breath. Now, chin on chest.'

'Pull up on your thighs, Lorraine.' Nicole came in. She just had time to swoop in and swab their patient's thighs with antiseptic. Dr Gilbert had put on gloves but wasn't wasting time on a gown.

'I can feel. . .I can feel. . .'

'That's right, Lorraine, the head's halfway out. OK, take a breath and push.'

The head was born, the baby's eyes closed and the little face oddly motionless. It was frightening to those who hadn't seen birth before, but perfectly normal, as Nicole knew. She quickly suctioned out the baby's mouth and nose so that there would be nothing to get in the way of the first breath.

'OK, stop pushing, Lorraine.' The cord was looped around the baby's neck and needed to be freed, which Richard Gilbert did deftly as Mrs Miller panted urgently once more.

Just before the next contraction attained its force he delivered the upper shoulder, and one more push brought the baby out. The little thing cried almost at once, a lusty bawl that had his mouth wide and his eyes screwed up in protest.

'Well, will you look at that?' Dr Gilbert said, grinning. 'It's a perfect boy, Lorraine.'

He placed the baby onto her stomach and she held him, laughing and crying and shaking. 'A boy! You and your "generic masculine"! And so easy!'

'What's his name?'

'Brian. Hello, Brian. Hello. Oh, if only Don had been here! Can the girls come in?'

But there was still a fair bit to do. The cord was clamped and cut, and Nicole had recorded the Apgar score at one minute and was waiting to do it again at five. The tiny Plexiglas warming bed arrived, delivered by an orderly as Dr Gilbert had ordered, and she laid the baby in it while Lorraine pushed again very gently to deliver the placenta, which came out fully intact.

The new mother was still emotional and exclaiming with delight, and Dr Gilbert was beaming, too, with a surprising softness around his dark eyes. Nobody would have guessed that it was his tenth baby since Friday.

Nicole, though, was thinking sadly, This is a treat for my first day. Such a treat! I'd forgotten how much I love these happy, *wanted* births, and I used to get to be a part of them every day before the accident. Still, I mustn't let her see. I mustn't spoil it and anyway, I still get to see all these happy pregnant ladies, and the babies as well if the mothers bring them in to their six-week post-partum check.

She brushed the unexpected sadness aside because Mrs Miller was now ready to see the little girls. As soon as they'd seen their new baby brother, Brian and his mother would be taken off to the maternity floor. She hadn't torn, or bled very much, and her uterus—Dr Gilbert was palpating it now—was already beginning to contract as it should.

Nobody noticed, Nicole decided. Thank goodness.

She was wrong.

'We put these little dramas on deliberately to test our new staff on their first day,' Richard Gilbert told her very seriously two hours later, when the day's last patient had belatedly departed and Mr Miller had arrived to pick up his daughters and take them through to the maternity floor. 'Lorraine Miller isn't a patient at all, just a very clever actress. We've used her several times now. And I think Brian has a big future in Hollywood, too, don't you?'

She laughed, not having expected humour from him after their bad start, then said, equally seriously, 'Do you think so? I didn't find that first cry at all convincing, I must say. Far too melodramatic to really convey the complex experience of entering the world.'

'Gee, tough audience, aren't you? Seriously, though. . .'

'Please tell me it *doesn't* happen every week!'

And suddenly he really was serious. 'Actually, I got the impression you'd be quite happy if it did. You miss it, don't you?'

'Being part of a successful birth? Oh, yes! I— Sorry, I didn't want it to show.'

'I don't think it did. Not to Lorraine, anyway. I. . . just happened to be watching you at the time, that's all.' There was a tiny pause, and then he said in a very smooth voice, 'And now can I drop you home to change? Our reservation is for six-thirty.'

'R-reservation?'

'Yes. Dinner. At the Refectory. Considered by some to be the best dining Columbus has to offer. Isn't that what you asked for?'

'Oh, Dr Gilbert, I was joking.'

'I know,' he drawled, 'but if you can call my bluff I can call yours. Unless you can offer me concrete evidence of other plans I'm holding you to what you said this morning, and I expect a certain degree of gratitude for my efforts at wangling a reservation at such short notice.'

There was a positively evil glitter in his dark eyes as he waited with very evident anticipation for her response to his provocative words. Nicole's chin lifted. She was well able to rise to such a challenge, especially when there was this quite electric charge in the air between them suddenly. She didn't understand it but felt its power.

'Gratitude?' she answered him. 'Certainly you have my gratitude, although six-thirty isn't exactly a fashionable hour for dining.'

'No,' he flashed back at once, 'but since I got an hour of sleep last night I felt entitled to call the shots on that issue.'

'If you're that tired I wouldn't dream of holding you to an elaborate meal,' she assured him sweetly.

'I've been in this business for over ten years, not counting medical school. I wouldn't have survived if I hadn't been able to rise above a touch of fatigue.'

'In that case, I'll be happy to join you for dinner tonight, Dr Gilbert.'

'It'll be my pleasure,' he drawled.

Behind the words, though, there was a dangerous sense that if she didn't perform as desired he would soon let her know it. This realisation ought to make her angry, surely, and yet it didn't because she had the strong impression that the particular performance he did desire from her was by no means the obvious one.

Intrigued and stimulated, she realised she could be playing with fire here. And what if she turned out to like it?

He dropped her home ten minutes later, having left the office suite to Cynthia, the office manager, to lock up. He needed to change himself, of course, as he was still wearing those rather striking and very muscle-moulding blue scrubs, and told Nicole casually, 'Six-fifteen. It's not a long drive.'

'That *may* give me enough time. I'm sure you wouldn't want me under-dressed.'

'I'm not convinced it would be possible for you to be under-dressed for anything, Ms Martin.'

She still hadn't worked out quite what he could have meant by *that* little sally when he disappeared around a corner at the end of the street.

Inside, she turned up Barb's heating a bit—this morning's snow was still lying intact on the ground, re-freezing as the day cooled after softening somewhat in the midday sun—then contemplated her strategy. Firstly, should she fulfil Richard Gilbert's expectations or attempt to defy them?

Just exactly what *were* his expectations, though? This evening was a form of punishment, it seemed, and that should really have made her angry. He'd certainly made her angry this morning, which was how she'd got into this situation in the first place.

The key, she finally decided, was to look as if she'd just flung something on but somehow ended up stunningly gorgeous all the same.

'Yeah, right,' she told the bathroom mirror in her best Australian imitation of a California 'valley girl' accent. 'Like *that's* easy!'

She had brought two dresses with her, and one of

them was definitely for summer. Which left the black one. After a shower, taken purely for procrastination purposes, she put it on, smoothed its figure-hugging curves over her slim hips and wasn't very satisfied. Even with gold jewellery, she thought it made her look as if she was taking the evening *far* too seriously!

Then she saw it—the Chinese silk shawl that Barb had hung on the wall in her bedroom, exquisitely bright with embroidered flowers in half a dozen hot colours and edged with a long, knotted silk fringe.

'Use anything in the house,' Barb had said, 'and I mean *anything*. If I didn't want it used I put it in storage.'

'Did she include wearing her wall decor in that statement?' Nicole asked Astro, but the ginger creature pointedly disdained the giving of advice on the issue, jumping off the bed to stalk silently from the room. 'I'll take that as a yes,' she decided, unhooking the fabric loops that attached the shawl and flinging the gorgeous garment gypsy-like around her bare shoulders.

She brushed her hair, un-brushed it again by flinging it around with her fingers, tossed in some combs, darkened her lashes, streaked her mouth with scarlet and decided very happily that she had done it. If she met him at the door ever so casually with a magazine still in her hand. . . She found one about thirty seconds before his knock sounded and just had time to open it and stick her thumb in, ostensibly to mark her place.

Wandering across to open the door, she was immediately greeted with, 'Is that all you're wearing?'

She forgot the magazine, which he'd never noticed at all. 'You said it wasn't possible for me to be underdressed.' It came out sounding very indignant.

'I meant a coat,' he explained patiently. 'It's cold out.'

Oops. Plum coat and scarlet shawl. Didn't go.

'Oh, I. . .won't bother, I don't think,' she answered airily. 'I don't feel the cold much.'

Then of course she had to hide the fact that she was

shivering until his car heater warmed up. So much for nonchalance. If he noticed, though, he didn't comment, which gave her the chance to notice *him*, and she realised with chagrin that he'd achieved just the look that she'd been after.

Dark, understated pants, an understated pale olive-brown shirt that looked like linen, a silk tie of the same colour and so understated it might have taken lessons in camouflage from a chameleon. . . It was infinitely easier for a man, of course. With his soft leather jacket flung open, he looked casual yet well groomed, and he smelled—She abruptly tried to change the direction of her thoughts. I'm hungry. I'll be eating soon. I won't notice that muskiness then. This isn't a 'date.' I can't go thinking he's gorgeous, or anything. That would be disastrous!

Alarmed at the direction in which her thoughts persisted in travelling, she wriggled and fussed in the passenger seat for a minute, adjusting the shawl—which had fallen off her shoulders—so that it looked as prim as could be until he said tersely, 'Is there something wrong?'

'No. . . Why?'

'You're fidgeting like a five-year-old. I can't concentrate on driving, and there might be some slippery patches. If you're cold just say so and I'll turn the heating up. Don't fuss with that shawl.'

'Sorry.'

'Here.' He reached out and deftly adjusted a lever or two so that hot air came roaring onto her bare knees.

She said meekly a few minutes later, 'That's much better. Thanks. I *was* cold.'

'I can't stand silent suffering when something can easily be fixed.'

'I'll remember that.'

'Do!' He was silent for a moment, then added, 'That applies at the office, too, by the way. Barb had her systems, but if there's anything you want to change. . .'

'Well, there was one thing.'

'Yes?' The monosyllable didn't exactly invite a radical proposition, but since this wasn't one. . .

'Is there any way I can let you know which patient you should see next? This morning you went in to Mrs Drake before you did Mrs Green's annual, and she'd been waiting longer. At Dr Hill's I always put the chart upright in the rack for the next patient and lying on its side for the one after.'

'Isn't that a nuisance for you?'

'Less so than having someone get forgotten, or having to stop you and turn you round when you've already got your hand on the door.'

'You're planning to spoil me.'

'I hate an untidy routine.'

'Don't know how you can stand that shawl, then, because it's *very* untidy. It's slipping again,' he muttered, and she fixed it quickly as he added, 'As for the system with the charts. . . Sure! Let's see how it works.'

He pulled into the restaurant car park, then warned her as they walked towards the low building that had once been a church, 'Watch out for the ice.'

She saw the patch he meant, pooled across their path and glistening in the last late light, and waited for him to take her arm as her spiky shoes were flagrantly impractical for anything resembling real walking. He didn't, though, and she was about to set off and skirt around it when belatedly he made the offer, holding out his forearm stiffly, deliberately over-formal. He even gave a tiny bow.

But he hated doing it. Nicole could see that, could *feel* it in the rigid rope of his arm muscles beneath the leather of his jacket which was so soft against her palm. Her thanks were therefore as frosty as the ice he was helping her to traverse.

'You must be a good six feet in those shoes,' he

accused bluntly, releasing her the moment they attained the safety of dry asphalt again.

'Yes. And I like it,' she answered, deliberately defiant. 'It makes *most* men think twice about asking me out.' Then she added rashly, 'Which you should have done if you were too tired to keep your temper!'

They looked at each other and she waited for the explosion, knowing she'd gone too far. The air crackled, his jaw bunched into two symmetrical knots, his brow folded into a black groove, his hands were poised at his sides. . .and then he laughed.

'OK,' he conceded. 'OK, Ms Martin.'

'Can't you make it Nicole?'

'Nicole. Sure. It's. . .nice.' She waited for him to suggest using his first name but he didn't, adding after a moment, 'Do you get Nicky?'

'Only from people I don't like!'

He laughed again. 'So if I feel the urge to abbreviate. . .'

'You'd better make it Nic. Otherwise, don't say you weren't warned!'

Inside the restaurant it was warm and dark and enticingly full of savoury aromas. Their meal was superb, and almost as elaborate as the pompous waiter's effusive descriptions made it sound.

'Do you think he gets paid by the word?' Dr Gilbert suggested quietly after they had ordered.

'I don't know about that, but *we* clearly pay by the mouthful!' She had gulped as she scanned the prices.

'We?'

'Well, you,' she conceded. 'You did insist on calling my bluff. Serves you right that it doesn't come cheap.'

'At the moment I'm not regretting it.'

'There's a veiled threat there, I detect.'

'No.' He controlled a stiff sigh. 'No, there isn't, Nicole.'

But there was something. . .

Four courses came and went, with wine and then coffee as accompaniments, and she couldn't work out just what was going on. They'd talk non-stop for ten minutes, sparkling floods of words, and the sardonic bite of his humour would tempt her into bold sallies that verged on danger more than once. He seemed to like it, though, until suddenly he'd frown and sit back in his chair, stop caressing the stem of his wine-glass in that absent way and once more get that irritated look she'd seen in his face this morning.

'What *is* it, Dr Gilbert?' she demanded finally.

Richard couldn't blame her for asking the question. The evening wasn't going at all according to plan, although most of the time he was enjoying himself too much to remember what the plan had been. He was definitely exhausted, which meant that although he was drinking only lightly—it was a superb Merlot, by the way—the heat that came from the nearby fire was relaxing him far too much. And he didn't *want* to relax. That wasn't the point of this. The point of it was to discover that Nicole Martin's resemblance to Linda was so superficial that it didn't matter.

And it *was* superficial, he realised confusedly. Ms Martin was nothing like Linda in essence. So, was that good or bad? Somehow he'd lost track of the programme here, lost track of his motives.

'Tired,' he told her belatedly, seizing on it as the easiest excuse.

'Let's go, then. I know you've got surgery tomorrow.'

She drained the last of her coffee and was on her feet a moment later. He liked this confidence in her, this decisiveness. Linda had had those traits too but far more brashly expressed, far more selfishly motivated.

Hang on. . . No! It was *way* too soon to conclude something like that about Nicole Martin. He rose as well. 'Yes. It's been a wonderful evening, though.' It was obligatory to say that. But he hadn't expected to mean it so much, and added tartly, 'And I hope it's taught you a valuable lesson.' He waited with a pleasurable anticipation for her biting response, and wasn't disappointed.

'That if I'm brazen and rude enough I can wangle an invitation to a really, really expensive restaurant from someone I barely know?' she clarified. 'Yes, I imagine that *could* be a valuable lesson. I'll let you know if I can get it to work on anyone else.'

'Do,' he agreed.

'And I'll give you a cut of the proceeds. A nice doggy bag of left-overs. . .'

He laughed, relishing her irreverence.

Nicole gathered up her shawl. Since it had appeared to irritate Dr Gilbert so much she had dropped it over the back of her chair during the meal and almost forgotten it. Now she felt a surge of sensory pleasure again as the cool silk slid on the bare skin of her arms and shoulders and the gorgeous folds fell almost to her knees.

Enveloped in the shimmering scarlet and yellow and pink, she felt as graceful and physical as a dancer and couldn't help smiling as they walked to the door. Dr Gilbert had retreated into himself once more so that as they left the restaurant they were both distracted and forgot about the treacherous ice near the car.

It was dark now, and there was nothing to reflect off that smooth, glossy black surface. She took one step onto it and realised at once what had happened, but it was too late. Her foot skated from under her, taking her weight with it, and if Dr Gilbert hadn't grabbed her unceremoniously around the waist, his strong hands crushing the silk of her shawl, she would have fallen.

He was on the ice as well, however, and it was slippery enough that even in his far sturdier shoes his footing was not secure. For a moment neither of them could move, teetering there, then he made a lunge for the edge of the ice, lifting her with him, but she wasn't prepared for the change of direction and arched backwards, stretching her back cruelly.

He realised instantly that she was in pain, took a concerned rasp of breath between his teeth and pulled her upright as soon as he was on solid ground so that she fetched up a scant two inches from him. As she approached his own height in those shoes, her nose bumped against his mouth, her lips against his chin and her breasts. . .

She gasped, he grunted, then both of them froze. This felt. . .wonderful.

Slowly, experimentally, his head bent just a little further and she knew that he was seeking her lips. Not hesitating, she gave him her mouth and they met in a kiss that was at once fiery and gentle, dangerously exciting and sweetly controlled. He was still supporting her back, splaying his hand against it right where the slippery folds of her shawl crossed her spine.

It was well below freezing but his bulk and the square shoulders of his leather jacket sheltered her so that she felt quite warm in his arms, especially when his other hand rose to caress the smooth knobs of her bare shoulders, making the thin straps of her dress threaten to slip off.

Next he touched her neck, and she could feel her pulses beating beneath his fingertips. Her breasts were throbbing now, too, peaking and tingling, and there was an electric connection that radiated from those tender buds all through her body. His mouth was harder on hers now, hungrier and more demanding, and her own response to him heightened by the minute. The sensation of it billowed and grew, swamping every sense. Touch, smell, taste. . .

She lifted her hands to hold them against the late-hour roughness of his face, then threaded them still higher into his thick mass of dark hair. Her eyes had closed instinctively but now she forced them open and saw the dilated blackness of his pupils beneath a blurred screen of lashes before his eyes closed, too, making his tired face look quite naked and abandoned so close to her own.

Her heart lurched sickly. She'd never experienced such an overpowering physical connection, hadn't had an inkling until his kiss that this was what all that instantly electric, hostile skirmishing between them had been about today. Now that she knew it was *this*, she didn't have a clue what to do about it. Having burst like the banks of a river in spate, would it just go away? Her relationship with Colin Cotterill, entered into when she was so vulnerable and ending so unpleasantly, had taught her nothing that was of any help now.

Breathlessly, she arched her neck to turn her mouth away from his and murmured all her confusion in one almost ludicrously prim phrase.

'Oh, Dr Gilbert. . .!'

CHAPTER THREE

WITH three medical students observing surgery this morning, Richard used the television monitor to view the procedure, which he didn't normally do. The operation was extremely routine—a bilateral tubal ligation on a well-informed thirty-five-year-old woman who had three children and didn't want any more.

Everything was going fine. The nurse-anaesthetist had put the patient under, the circulating and scrub nurses were completely efficient and cheerful as usual and he'd given himself easy access to the Fallopian tubes by blowing up the abdominal cavity with a good four litres of carbon dioxide. He had the cautery in his hand, ready to lift the tubes clear and burn the tissue, and that was when it happened.

He looked at that television screen in all its living colour and for one horrible moment nothing that he saw made any sense because it had suddenly struck him out of the blue. She called me Dr Gilbert. We were kissing like crazy and it was fabulous—which I didn't want—and then she called me Dr Gilbert, as if we barely knew each other. And she's right, of course. We do. Or don't, I mean. Don't know each other at all. . .

He blinked, still having to grimly fight fatigue after the heavy weekend on call, and stared at the screen again. What *was* that? What on earth was it? That pink cavern with the yellow rocks in the foreground, and that domed, shiny—

The uterus. It clicked back into place, and his heart slowed to the right rhythm again after several panicky beats. Glancing at the nurses and the medical students, he knew with relief that the whole episode could only have lasted a second or two. None of them had noticed.

In control again, he eased the yellow rocks out of the way. 'Fat,' he told the students. 'And this is the bowel, of course. The uterus. The ovaries. Here's the tube.'

He lifted it, lost it briefly—it was slippery and stretchy and attached to a membrane—then lifted it again and pressed the two metal fingers of the cautery together, turning the tube white and then, in patches, brown.

He had time to think grimly, Last night was a complete failure, then, as far as my stated objectives were concerned.

Then he carefully lifted the second tube and burned it as well. The tissue was dead now, and would eventually disappear, leaving a gap which—seventy per cent of the time—could later be bridged successfully if the woman had a change of heart.

In contrast to the initial ligation, however, it was a delicate, time-consuming and expensive procedure, and he did everything he could to discourage his patients from regarding 'having their tubes tied' as a reversible option. Human beings were fickle creatures, though. He'd referred two patients to microsurgeon, Anne Kennedy, in the past year for the procedure, and one of them was pregnant already.

Still, in view of last night's anomalous—no, quite *illogical*—behaviour on his part, he wasn't exactly in a position to criticise any perceived fickleness in his patients.

I'll ask her out again. That's the only solution, he concluded irritably. And *this* time. . .

'We didn't get much of a chance to talk yesterday when Darla whisked you through my office,' Elaine Bridgman said to Nicole as she propelled her wheelchair through the lab area to the small alcove where patients were weighed, 'but I know Barb was looking forward to her exchange immensely, and I hope you'll have as good a time with us. We all like Dr Gilbert, but he does have high standards.'

'So do I,' Nicole answered firmly, fighting her blush as she forcefully pushed last night to the back of her mind. He would be here any minute.

Elaine worked in the practice's billing office, but this morning she was taking the first appointment of the day with Dr Gilbert—a routine prenatal exam at the halfway point in her pregnancy. She had been in an accident five years previously and had a spinal cord injury just above the T6 level—the sixth of the twelve thoracic vertebrae.

This was her first pregnancy and so far, apparently, she hadn't had many problems at all. She found it more difficult than usual to insert her urinary catheter and had greater trouble transferring, manoeuvring and bending, but dealt with these difficulties cheerfully and was happy to be past the twenty-week milestone in her pregnancy.

Her husband was due to meet her here, and, yes, here he was now, a tall and rather lanky man with owlish spectacles and a beguiling grin.

'Hi, Paul,' Elaine said. 'Nicole's ready to weigh me now, so can we do it the usual way?'

'It's what I'm here for,' he answered cheerfully, stepping onto the scales as he spoke.

Nicole frowned, then said, 'Oh, you mean I'm going to have to do some arithmetic?'

'I'll help,' Paul Bridgman said. 'I'm an engineer.'

He tipped the scales at 192 pounds, which sounded like a vast figure to Nicole, who was used to metric measurements. Then he stepped off again and swung his wife confidently into his arms so that her long fall of dark, straight hair cascaded across his arm.

She giggled and kissed his neck, giving a smile that wrinkled her button nose. 'Lucky he has a strong back.'

This time Nicole had to move the marker on the scale until it dipped at 318 and she was still desperately trying to resurrect her rusty mental arithmetic skills when Paul came to her rescue. 'One twenty-six,' he said as he put Elaine back in the chair.

Nicole noted down the figure. A total gain of eleven pounds, which was quite acceptable for this point in the pregnancy.

'Urine sample now?' Elaine asked.

'Yes. Do you need help? Dr Gilbert's out of surgery, but he had post-partum rounds and an induction to start so you've got a few minutes.'

'It's probably quicker if I do it myself, anyway.'

She manoeuvred herself into the bathroom and Paul closed the door for her, then turned immediately to Nicole, the easy-going expression dropping instantly from his face.

'Is it really going OK, do you think?' he demanded in a low voice. 'I'm so damned scared of this. . . I just can't help having a bad feeling about it. She wants it so much. She works so hard at not letting her disability make a difference in our lives. If anything goes wrong. . . We got through the accident without having it break us apart—my father was driving, he was at fault and he was killed—but if anything went wrong with this baby. . .'

'Oh, Paul. . .' Nicole felt swamped by his sudden need for assurances. She knew about accidents, knew how they could bind people together or tear them apart. Sometimes both. Like herself and Colin. If they hadn't been in the accident together. . .

She shuddered.

But Elaine and Paul had weathered their accident and its aftermath and, remembering the very normal details of Elaine's chart—including the results of tests done for birth defects on her last visit—she said truthfully, 'There's absolutely no reason to think that Elaine will have any more trouble because of her spinal cord injury than a woman who's not disabled. Hasn't Dr Gilbert told you that?'

'Every visit.' Paul laughed ruefully. 'Sorry. I guess I'm asking the impossible. I want an iron-clad promise.'

They heard the toilet flush, and at once he schooled away the tension in his face. 'I just have to wait, don't I?' he had time to mutter, then his wife emerged, having left her urine sample in the wall-box which opened on the other side to the lab where Nicole immediately tested it.

Negative for sugar, and with just a trace of protein. Quite normal, in other words, as was her blood pressure, at 116 over 68, a minute later.

If Elaine was feeling the same fears as her husband she wasn't letting them show. She sat there, smiling, as she told Nicole, 'Dr Gilbert wants to do an ultrasound at twenty-eight weeks and then start seeing me weekly after that, just to be on the safe side. We haven't decided yet if we'll let him tell us the sex, have we, Paul?'

'Whatever you want, babe,' he told her, running his hand down the heavy fall of shining dark hair.

'Well, seeing Dr Gilbert every day and knowing that *he* knows. . . On the other hand, I'd like to be surprised, too.'

'Make up your mind, woman,' Paul growled.

'I've got another six weeks.'

'That's what I'm afraid of, having you swing like a weather vane every day for six more weeks.'

Elaine just laughed.

'Take room three,' Nicole told them now, slotting Elaine's chart upright into the Plexiglas holder beside the door. 'Dr Gilbert will see you as soon as he gets in. Just a tummy check today so you don't need to undress. If there's any delay I'll let you know.'

Impulsively she patted Paul's arm as he followed his

wife inside, and then she shut the door behind the couple, thinking, It *has* to work out for them, surely! They seem so strong together. I can't imagine what that's like, to be so connected yet without it turning suffocating and possessive and horrible. I don't think I could ever stand it. It's certainly not what I can imagine wanting in the foreseeable future. So perhaps it was all in me, not in Colin at all. . .

But in her heart she knew that wasn't true.

Thinking this as she went out to the waiting room to call in the other nine forty-five appointment, she almost cannoned into Richard Gilbert as he rounded the corner of the cream and sage-green corridor.

'Steady!' It came out dark, with a little catch of huski-ness. He touched her lightly on the arms and she felt the brief fan of his breath against her hair.

Her body coiled with the memory of last night's kiss and she knew her heart was beating faster as she looked up at him, smiling, and managed a rather breathy, 'Hi!'

But if she'd expected to see anything special in his face. . . That look of edgy irritation was back, and stronger than ever, too, creasing his brow and making his dark eyes glitter. She felt her own mouth tighten into the same shape as his.

'Room three?' was all he said.

'Yes, it's Elaine. She checked out with no problems at my end.'

'Great. . . And I see we've started the system of the upright charts.'

'Yes, if you like it.'

'I'm sure I will.'

He brushed past her and disappeared into the examining room.

She called the next patient, knowing she must look flushed and having to struggle a little to put the thing in perspective. So he clearly regarded their kiss—the whole evening, perhaps—as a mistake. OK. With her own history, the last thing she wanted to do was tie herself in knots about it, invade his space if she wasn't wanted there—*pester* him. He needn't look so grumpy about the whole thing, though!

She spent the rest of the week trying to let him see this. She pointedly avoided even the slightest nuance of physical contact, keeping an object between herself and him for mutual protection at all times—even if it was merely the flimsy manila rectangle of a patient's chart— and resisting the sometimes mighty impulse to indulge in any of those biting rejoinders which had got her into so much trouble on Monday.

And she was just beginning to feel a satisfactory sense that the problem had gone away since he'd been looking less irritated over the past day or two when, on Friday at lunch-time, he confounded her understanding of the issue utterly by asking her out again.

Or asking her *home*, rather, to dinner at his place that very night.

She resisted her initial urge to give explosive vent to her bewilderment by telling him just what he could do with his home-cooked meal. She resisted a petulant need to disdain the short notice he had given her of the event. Finally, she resisted the temptation to create a prior engagement. One of the other nurses, Gretchen Cain, had vaguely mentioned a movie and a hamburger, but nothing had come of it yet and she didn't want to get caught out in a lie.

This is for you, Barb, she finally decided, so that Dr Gilbert and I won't have a completely miserable year together and make him furious with you for proposing this exchange.

He was waiting for her answer, typically impatient, and as she knew he was about to head off to Labor and Delivery to rupture a membrane—she suspected the

labouring woman might be getting a bit impatient, too,
as she'd been in since yesterday afternoon—she told
him briefly at last, 'Yes, I'm free. What time would you
like me?'

'Unfortunate way of putting it,' he muttered, 'but,
OK, I'd like you at seven. If that suits.'

'It suits fine.'

'Good.'

He skulked off to Labor and Delivery and was back
again within minutes to eat a pizza lunch, closeted
grumpily in his office. His patient then delivered most
conveniently at ten past four, just after his last appointment for the day. He had no one else in labour and he
wasn't on call this weekend.

And if that doesn't put him in a good mood, then I
can't imagine what will! Nicole thought. Nonetheless,
she was going to play it as safe as she could.

After Monday's snow, and a temperature that hadn't
risen above freezing, the mercury today, four days later,
had topped seventy-two degrees Fahrenheit. Rather
bizarre, Nicole considered, although Darla Hogan told
her that it was quite normal for Columbus. 'If you don't
like the weather here, people say, stick around for five
minutes 'cos it'll change. Actually, that usually means
it gets worse, but today. . .'

'Gorgeous,' Nicole agreed.

And it meant she could wear the other dress, the pretty
floral summer one. With plenty of time and a hunger
for that lovely sun, she walked down to High Street in
search of a bottle of wine to bring, then wended her
way through the quiet streets of Northmoor to reach his
place while it was still light and warm.

He was wearing close-fitting faded jeans now, a blue
chambray shirt rolled to the elbows and expensive running shoes that gave him the silent, springy tread of a
mountain lion. And he was barbecuing.

'The one area of cuisine in which I am remotely

skilled,' he declared, but as he brandished a long, gleaming two-pronged fork in one hand and a rapier-like skewer in the other in order to turn the seasoned chicken breasts she began to suspect he'd chosen the menu largely for the sake of the weaponry it afforded him.

Between the violent sizzle of the white meat on the grill directly in front of him and the rapacious cut and thrust of the fork and skewer, Nicole felt not the remotest desire to break her employer's personal boundaries. Instead, she perched herself several yards away on the railing of his wooden patio deck, sipping her crisply chilled wine and enjoying the sunset over the late winter garden. It really was ridiculously mild, considering that the daffodils were not yet out and the trees were bare of even the faintest green.

He threw a plate of corn chips and a bowl of Mexican salsa in her direction, with the brusque warning, 'It's a fiery one. Sorry, I don't have anything milder.'

'The spicier the better, as far as I'm concerned,' she told him, 'although it does tend to numb the lips.'

'Don't worry, I'm not planning to kiss you.'

'And I'm not planning to *be* kissed so we've got that settled.'

'Apparently.'

They sniped at each other for the rest of the evening until, after the mouth-wateringly savoury chicken, they were both on a slow boil. When they moved inside for coffee Nicole decided that he *was* going to kiss her. Not that she'd even begin to let him after what he'd said about it! He deserved a bit of punishment for—

For what? Giving her the second most enjoyable evening she'd spent in a long time? Or did this one actually top Monday's event? She felt confused in a rather delicious way, admitting to herself finally that all those sarcastic little comments on her part and biting responses on his were as enticing and exciting as any more physical foreplay, and wondered why they both seemed to need this.

He *was* going to kiss her. She was sure of it now. She wanted it too, but was very content to play the traditional female role and wait to see how he would manage it. There was a zest to him, a deeply rooted capability. She knew the last thing he would do would be to make it clumsy or crass.

So, when he didn't kiss her at all, she was left. . . quite unfairly *peeved*.

He'd had plenty of opportunity. He'd even driven her the short distance home. But when he pulled up outside her house he left the engine running, which was a hint if ever there was one, and he sat so stiffly at the wheel that she might have been tempted to laugh at the pomposity of it—only somehow there was nothing remotely pompous about Richard Gilbert in any of his roles. Doctor, barbecue guru. . .

Lover? she wondered, and there came to her unbidden a sudden treacherous image of his male nakedness. Suppressing it almost before it had formed, she accepted that somehow she'd been totally wrong, wrong, *wrong* about whatever electricity she had been so sure she'd sensed between them, and ejected herself from his car with the speed of a cork popping from a bottle—only remembering to give appropriate thanks at the last possible moment.

'My pleasure,' he drawled, scarcely even attempting to make it sound sincere.

She alternated between fuming and shrugging about it the whole weekend. On Saturday the weather stayed mild and Darla invited her on a family picnic to Highbanks Metro Park and then on Sunday, which was a revisitation of winter, Gretchen came good with her movie and hamburger idea. In between these events Nicole explored on foot and by car, stocked up on food supplies and wrote to her parents so it wasn't as if she just sat around and was *obsessed* over the wretched Richard. . .

'Which is what I might just call him from now on!' she said aloud.

Still, though, the man persisted in occupying a significantly larger place in her thoughts than she was happy with.

And then on Monday it was back to work. He was called to a delivery—twins—almost at once, and as his first four patients then elected to go off and do errands to fill in time before their delayed appointments she did the initial prenatal nursing interview that Gretchen had been scheduled to do, as the latter had been held up with car trouble.

Twenty-one-year-old Samantha Clay was chirpy and ecstatic about her pregnancy, and it was only some minutes into the rather long series of questions which would produce a detailed patient history that it became apparent that she might not be pregnant after all. She'd missed her period three weeks ago, but had had irregularities in the past. When asked how she was feeling, she said, 'Great! Isn't that how pregnant women are supposed to feel? Ripening, you know. New life? Bursting with energy?'

'Not usually in the first trimester,' Nicole answered. 'Most women find they're very tired.'

'Well, I've been sleeping a fair bit, I guess. I'm only taking one class at Ohio State this quarter. Mike's got a good job, though, so we decided we could afford a baby.'

'But the pregnancy test you did was positive?'

'Well, I haven't actually done a test. I mean, what else could it be? We stopped using contraception last month, and bingo!'

'Let's do a test,' Nicole said firmly.

Samantha was a patient of Dr Kramer's, and the tall,

elegant brunette with her incredibly demanding schedule—including three young children of her own—
wouldn't appreciate doing a first prenatal exam on this
young woman next week only to find that she wasn't
pregnant at all.

A specimen was produced and Nicole started the
test, then ducked out of the lab to take a call from Dr
Gilbert.

'Nicole? Safely delivered, both of them. Two girls. I
should be there in fifteen.'

'OK, I'll have patients ready.'

Back in the lab Darla was hovering over the pregnancy test, frowning heavily.

'Is that Samantha Clay's?'

Darla looked up and made a face. 'No, it's mine!'

'Oh, are you—?' Nicole began eagerly.

Darla picked up the testing stick. The tiny square at
the end of it remained most definitely white. 'No, I'm
not. . . Thank goodness!' She flourished the stick and
then tossed the test in the garbage. 'I have three beautiful
kids, and that's enough.' Then she laughed. 'But it's an
occupational hazard in this job, I find, thinking I might
be. I know all the symptoms off by heart, and can always
imagine I have at least one of them. I have a pregnancy
scare about every three months!'

'And Gretchen was telling me that she suffers from
the *other* occupational hazard of Ob nurses—getting
clucky.'

'Yes, no doubt about it, it's a dangerous job!'

'So far, I've been immune to both ailments,' Nicole
said lightly. 'But, meanwhile, where's the pregnancy
test I was doing for Mrs Clay?'

'Oh, that? Positive. *Very* positive. Quite purple.'

'That's a relief! I can get on with her prenatal,
then.'

She just had time to finish her list of questions and
usher Dr Gilbert's first patient into an examining room

before he appeared, making a blue scrubsuit look far sexier than it ought to, at which point Darla's phrase came back to her. 'Occupational hazard.' Every job had one, perhaps. In this job, it looked more and more likely that that hazard was going to be him.

Richard moved the ultrasound probe across the pale, lubricated abdomen of his patient to find the first foetus again. Twins. His day had begun with them, and now was ending that way, too. This time, though. . .

Mrs Benjamin was saying, a little dazed, 'I wish Scott was here. His father's a twin, but I never thought. . .'

Richard wasn't listening. He couldn't. Moving that probe back and forth across one tiny foetus and then the other—little more than embryos at, he judged, about seven weeks' gestation, perhaps a touch more—he was hoping against hope that he'd see what he was looking for on the grey, grainy screen—the blurred pulsing of tiny heartbeats.

But as the seconds passed he couldn't find it on either of them.

He calculated dates again. These babies should be at eight weeks and five days' gestation but they didn't look it, and when he measured the crown-rump length he knew he was right. Those heartbeats had never got going, and the foetuses had ceased to be viable about ten days ago. Mrs Benjamin hadn't yet realised that anything was wrong. . .

Yes, she had. She'd stopped talking, lifted her head from the table and looked at him. Perhaps she'd asked him something requiring an answer and his silence had alerted her.

'It's. . .it's OK, isn't it?' she said, suddenly tense in every limb.

He hated this moment and cleared his throat before saying carefully, 'I'm afraid not. I should be seeing heartbeats and I'm not. The babies aren't viable, I'm afraid.'

It took several minutes for her to accept it, and he wished badly that she had her husband here for support. She was an intelligent woman, and when he explained how accurately it was possible to size and date a foetus at this age it made sense to her. By her dates, those little grey shapes should have been bigger, and even if her dates were wrong the crown-rump measurement he was getting meant that heartbeats should have been distinctly visible. She understood.

It was her first pregnancy, and he wanted to tell her, Don't worry. You'll conceive again and next time it'll be fine. The odds were vastly in her favour for this to be the case, but that probably wouldn't help now. It was this loss she needed to mourn first.

And then, of course, his pager started off. He knew who it would be. Alison Gorman was ready to deliver, and this was her second so it would probably go fast.

He told Mrs Benjamin, 'I'll schedule you for a D and C. Otherwise you might have to wait weeks for something to happen, and when it did there'd be a lot of cramping and bleeding, as it was twins.'

She nodded, trying not to cry. He opened the door of the ultrasound room and called urgently, 'Nicole?' He saw her striding towards him on those long, strong, slender legs.

'Your delivery?' she said.

'Yes, but, look, go in to Mrs Benjamin, would you?' He explained the situation and saw the concern in her face. 'Schedule the D and C with her, OK? My list is full for tomorrow morning. Don't know if there's a slot for me later in the week. Make it at lunchtime, if you have to. I won't have a woman kept waiting for something like this—it's too unfair.'

She nodded. 'Tomorrow lunch, then?'

'If you can.'

His pager sounded again and he had to leave. He found that he had complete confidence in Nicole Martin to handle Mrs Benjamin with sensitivity, though, and that would have surprised him if he'd taken her brash manner towards himself seriously. But he hadn't, of course, knowing he was at least equally to blame for their prickly skirmishings. It must still be, even after more than a week, her resemblance to Linda.

The delivery was routine—not to the Gormans, of course, but they didn't need him to gush, wrapped up as they were in their new son—and he was soon back in the office with no more patients to see but all the paperwork of the day to finish off as well as that sheaf of mail he hadn't had a chance to get to yet, stuck in the slot outside his office door.

He took it, shut himself away and had just begun to leaf through the notes of thanks from happy new parents—which he still enjoyed receiving—when the phone rang and it was—of all people, after more than six months of silence—Linda.

'Just an impulse,' she drawled. 'My therapist thinks I should go with my impulses at the moment.'

'And does your therapist think I should support you in that endeavour?' he returned with an edge, and then suddenly, as if a mist had cleared, he realised he didn't care any more.

She talked on—*rattled* on, he'd have said, if he'd been predisposed to unkindness—but he didn't even care enough to be unkind. She was an attractive, intelligent, successful and sophisticated woman. She just wasn't for him, and all those years when he'd been trying to persuade her into the mould of an appropriate life-partner for an obstetrician. . .well, he was as much to blame as she was, perhaps, for the fact that it hadn't happened.

He'd been asking something of her that she didn't

even *want* to provide and, caught up in establishing this ambitious practice, it had taken him too long to see it. He had kidded himself for so long, all through those years of separate dwellings, separate finances, separate interests, separate friends—so much separateness that in the end, when the law firm of Webley Furnass in Los Angeles had poached her from a smaller Columbus firm, her departure had scarcely left a hole in his schedule. He'd missed her, though. . .

Only he suddenly realised now that it wasn't *her* at all—it was the future promise of a loving marriage, shared interests, children. It was *absurd* that he wasn't yet married and a father. It was almost a professional liability. A man in this field of speciality nowadays already took five times as long as a woman did to build a practice, without the added handicap of being single.

Well, in five years he'd built his practice, as the senior physician in Riverbank Ob/Gyn, but his lack of a fatherly aura still made him uncomfortable at times. A male obstetrician needed to be able to say reassuringly to his patients, 'Yes, when my wife was in labour with our first, she. . .'

Only now, seeing clearly, he wondered how he ever could have intended Linda to fit that role. When she ended the call some minutes later he laughed aloud. 'I hope her therapist will be suitably pleased!'

He sat back in his chair and suddenly felt totally free. Free of Linda, free of the past. . .free, he realised, of his problem with Nicole Martin. So what if she looked like Linda? It didn't matter. His attraction towards her existed quite independently of that, and it was clear to him now that he could pursue it for the healthiest and best of reasons and not because he was trying to recapture Linda or because he was trying to escape her. She was simply altogether irrelevant.

And since he felt quite certain that there was a strong

element of very attractive sexual tension in Nicole's combativeness towards him. . .

He laughed again. He'd had more than a week in which to act since that magic moment when he'd first seen her in a sparkling curtain of falling snow and, their two dinners together notwithstanding, he'd wasted that week completely. There would be no more such inefficiency.

CHAPTER FOUR

'WOULD you like to phone your husband, Mrs Benjamin?' Nicole asked, distressed by this crisply dressed career woman's release of emotion.

'Yes, please.' She glanced at a delicate gold wrist-watch. 'He'll still be at work, but I don't care. I should have had him come in the first place, only I was determined to be so *efficient* about this pregnancy. I was actually planning to go back to the office after my appointment. What was I? Crazy?'

She dabbed at streaked make-up with a soggy tissue and lifted a Styrofoam coffee-cup to her mouth with a shaking hand.

Nicole made the call and then they waited fifteen minutes. All the other appointments were finished for the day and the staff were leaving. Dr Kramer had to take her children to the dentist. Gretchen had tidied all the examining rooms on the north side of the office suite. Nicole herself was behind now. She hadn't got her speculums in the autoclave or her charts down to the chart room.

But Mrs Benjamin seemed comfortable about being left alone now so she quietly got to work on these tasks, and then Mr Benjamin arrived and the couple left amid more tears. Earlier, Nicole had got on the phone and managed to schedule the D and C for tomorrow lunch-time, which would at least hasten the return to normal of Mrs Benjamin's hormones.

'I still feel so pregnant,' she had sobbed. 'Nauseous and tired and everything smelling funny, and yet I know now that really I'm *not*.'

Just after the Benjamins left, while she was pulling

54

fresh paper sheeting down from the roll in room two, Nicole heard Richard Gilbert arrive back from his delivery, but he disappeared immediately into his very comfortable, very masculine office and closed the door. She thought she'd seen the last of him for the day until, just as she was switching off the light, in the little alcove where she took blood pressures and talked to patients, he emerged.

His step was zesty and his dark face alive—until he caught sight of her, at which point there was suddenly an odd pause as if a tape had got stuck for a second in the video player. He stopped with his hand on the door, gave an abrupt, 'Oh,' then closed it carefully behind him and added, 'I thought you'd have gone.'

'Mrs Benjamin was pretty upset. Her husband came to take her home. I did get her scheduled for tomorrow lunchtime, though. Um. . .' He was still standing there. Watching her. 'How was your delivery?'

'No problems. A boy. Big! Come to my place and we'll go for a walk and get Chinese and talk about something other than obstetrics.'

She laughed, not knowing if he was serious—not believing he could be—and yet, taking a closer look, she saw that he was, which confused and stupefied her enough to blurt, 'Why, Dr Gilbert?'

'Why not?'

She was angry now. 'That's not an answer. On Friday I got the distinct feeling you were quite sorry you'd ever burdened yourself with my company, and now you're doing it again. You really don't have to. I can make my own life here socially, you know, just as I'm sure Barb intends to do in Sydney. I'm sure she's not expecting Dr Hill to—'

'Nicole, this has nothing to do with Barb or with duty.' He came towards her, moving confidently, the pale blue scrubs he wore today rippling softly on his hard male frame. The sight made her ache in places she didn't realise *could* ache.

'Then what does it have to do with?' she said, and could hear how betrayingly thin her voice sounded.

He loomed over her now and all at once she was violently and unmistakably aware of the shared electricity between them, almost as if he wanted her to be. He did. It was there in his face—in his crooked smile and in the slow smoulder which had ignited behind his dark eyes.

'You know,' he growled. 'You just *know*, don't you?'

'I—I thought I did,' she answered confusedly, able only to be honest, although she knew it was a huge betrayal of the way her body was reacting. 'But then on Friday—'

'Hell, look, you bear a striking resemblance to my former girlfriend, all right?' he told her abruptly. 'At first I considered that unfortunate and it put a lot of fight into me where this. . .us. . .was concerned, but now I've realised it doesn't matter. Linda and I— Our relationship was—' He broke off and she could see him closing in on the precise phrase he wanted.

She remembered what Darla had said last Monday about what she knew of the relationship with this Linda woman—they'd led very separate lives, there hadn't been much commitment—and came in with new, eager confidence, 'Look, if you're afraid I'm going to get clingy and demanding and possessive you've got absolutely nothing to worry about.'

'Haven't I?'

'No! That sort of cloying claustrophobia is the very *last* thing I want in a relationship. I'm not looking for commitment. Not at all. I want something that's warm and well balanced and *fun*. Most of all, fun. I mean, I'm here for a year. That's not long, and I really, really don't want to spend it in getting serious!'

There was a beat of silence. 'What makes you

think—? Or rather,' he amended carefully, 'how did you know I don't want a commitment?'

'Darla mentioned Linda last week. And your relationship, and the fact that it was...well, fairly open. Which, as I'm saying, is exactly what I want, too.'

Again there was the very briefest of pauses, then he drawled in an odd tone, 'It's refreshing to find a woman so sure of her needs.'

'Sorry...' She bit her lip. 'I went on a bit just then.'

'Don't apologise. You put your cards on the table. Every single one of them. I appreciate it.'

'And it's got rid of that qualm of yours, I hope,' she said rather awkwardly. He wasn't reacting quite as she'd expected.

Only now he did, saying, 'Oh, yes...' He covered the last yard between them and took her confidently into his arms to hold his mouth deliberately just a teasing half-inch from her own.

He murmured, 'Too many women won't say it, won't be upfront about the fact that the only thing they want from a relationship is raw sex. I find it...quite electrifyingly exciting that you're prepared to be so honest and I very much look forward to getting our relationship onto that footing as soon as we possibly can.'

She stiffened, suddenly alarmed, and her eyes widened. That wasn't what she'd meant, was it? Did no commitment instantly translate into immediate sex and nothing else? It—it didn't sound very *romantic*, somehow, although perhaps 'romantic' wasn't a word that should be used in this context. She frowned and stared down for a moment, too preoccupied to be aware of his close, intent scrutiny.

But to backtrack now? she was thinking. And, anyway, what alternative did she envisage? Perhaps there wasn't one, in which case...

'Y-yes,' she answered, not quite steadily, almost against his mouth, which had drifted even closer. 'It sounds great. It *is* great. . .to be so honest and open.'

Darting her gaze up at him, she saw an odd light of satisfaction glowing in his dark eyes. 'So that's what it's to be, then, is it? Sex, total sex and nothing but sex.'

'Well. . .'

'That is to say, if we should happen to find that there are other aspects of each other's company we enjoy—'

'Yes, oh, definitely,' she came in decisively, quite relieved. 'There's nothing that says we can't talk. . . or. . .or. . .um. . .I swim for my back, and I hike a fair bit, for example.'

'There you are, then,' he agreed smoothly. 'Two happy coincidences of interest right there. But we'll see, of course. It may turn out that we'll find the elemental physical bond quite sufficient.'

'Y-yes.' Sufficient? At the moment it was far too overpowering to be called merely sufficient.

He was still holding her lightly, one hand resting on the soft swell of her hip and the other across her back. Cynthia was still tidying up in the distant front office, and Dr Turabian was shut in his office way on the other side of the nurses' lab. It felt as if they were alone, in other words, and wouldn't it have been natural, in view of what they'd just agreed—in view of what she, at least, was feeling like a flood all through her—for him to kiss her?

He didn't, though, unless you could count that whisper-light brush of his mouth across hers that was over before it had begun. He released her and said in a brisk, businesslike way, 'Shall we go, then?'

'G-go?' There was something about his manner which was still making her *very* uneasy right now.

'Yes. Didn't we agree? My place, a walk, Chinese and not talking about obstetrics. And then, to cap the evening. . .'

He didn't finish but it was clear what he meant and she broke out in a cold sweat at the same moment that her knees went weak. It wasn't possible, surely, to feel like this! One part of her wanted it intensely—the sensation of his hands running hotly across her body, the solid maleness of him beneath her own fingers and seized in clawing handfuls as they approached a wild, shared climax. . .

But the rest of her was consumed by the silent inner panic of knowing that it was far, far too soon for her. She didn't just jump into bed with men she'd known for a week. She seemed to have set herself up for this, however, and to go all coy on the subject now. . .

'Oh, right,' she made herself say, as brisk and businesslike as he had been. 'That plan you suggested. I've got the car, though, and I'd like to change.'

'Well, obviously. . .'

He glanced down at his own scrubs, well seasoned after the long day, and she couldn't resist teasing, 'This was totally inevitable, I suppose, wasn't it? There's nothing sexier than a man who comes to work every day in his pyjamas!'

He grinned. 'Do you like them? I change colours for variety. I used to wear real clothes in the office but I spent so much time nipping in and out of the bathroom before and after every delivery and every surgery that I started to feel like Superman. I'm a doctor, not a bank manager, so I dress like a doctor now. No one's ever complained.'

'And I certainly won't.'

She meant it, too, and for the first time, when she thought of the probability that she would soon be sleeping with this man, she felt. . .weak, pulsing, on fire. She felt *all* of it, quite overpoweringly, not afraid of it at all.

They separated after emerging from the lift as their cars were parked in opposite directions, and she knew her heart was beating much faster than normal as she told him, trying to sound very casual, 'See you in a while, then.'

'I'm curious. . .'

'Yes, Richard?' It was the first time she had called him that, and the word—his name—felt deliciously right in her mouth, distracting her from his opening gambit.

He noticed, too, and cocked his head to one side to study her with a smile. 'Does it work for you, calling me that?'

'Think so. Shall I practise?'

'Sure.'

'Oh, Richard. . . Ri-chard? *Richard*!' Angrily, questioningly, operatically.

They were walking along the bike path through the park by the river, and she was starting to discover an odd, unexpected beauty in the still leaf-bare trees of this mid-western landscape, their dark branches etched against the grey-white sky. It was late, the temperature just below freezing, and there were few people about, just an odd roller-blader or jogger or dog-walker, so she felt free to sing and shout his name like that.

He laughed. 'Can you whisper it?'

'Psst! Richard!'

'No, not like that, Nic. The way you'd whisper it if we'd just made love.'

'Oh.'

'No?'

'M-maybe I'm not that good an actress, and you'll have to wait for the real thing.' Which sounded more provocative than she'd intended so she prompted quickly, to quench the glint in his eye, 'But you were curious, you said?'

'Yes. Just idly so. I'm wondering. . .' He seemed to be choosing his words carefully or was he just absorbed in helping her negotiate the patch of half-frozen mud and slush that covered the bike path at this point? 'I'm wondering whether there's any specific reason why, at such a relatively youthful and generally idealistic age, you've formed such a strong philosophical objection to the notion of commitment in a relationship, that's all.'

'Oh, it's not philosophical. It's purely personal,' she returned quickly, then realised too late that the convoluted wording of his question had drawn a far more revealing response from her than she was happy with.

And the fact that he immediately seized on it told her that he'd been hoping for just such a slip. 'So you don't object to commitment in other people's relationships, just your own?'

'Yes,' was all she could say.

'Why, Nicole?'

Here it was. The thing she hated talking about, hated even thinking about. The thing that made her feel so claustrophobic she'd come halfway around the world to try and clear the murky cobwebs of unpleasant memory from her head.

'Nothing very dramatic,' she lied lightly. 'I was engaged once and it wasn't fun, that's all.'

'Not fun,' he echoed thoughtfully. 'So much so that from that day forward you vowed to forever eschew any conduct that risked leading to a repetition of that fettered circumstance?'

'No, there was no vow,' she answered slowly, unable to rise to his light mood, let alone his florid vocabulary. 'I just. . .know I need space, that's all.'

She half expected him to keep prodding but, rather surprisingly, he didn't, steering her off the path so that they were tramping in silence through a small group of gnarled crab-apple trees and then across the grass of the playing fields towards a tree-lined creek.

It gave her time to think and inevitably she did, reliving it all again and shivering when she thought of the possibility that it could have ended even more horribly than it had.

It was two years ago now since she and Colin Cotterill had been driving home from a movie late at night and had been hit side-on by a drunk driver.

'I feel so badly to blame,' Colin had said innumerable times afterwards, although he hadn't been to blame at all.

Nicole had told him so, but he'd kept saying it and she'd realised after a while—she'd had plenty of time to think in hospital for four months as her spinal injury had healed—that what he'd really felt had been the guilt of the survivor. He'd walked away from the accident, while she had been lucky ever to walk again. If that chipped piece of bone in her spine had cut in a fraction of an inch more deeply her spinal cord would have been severed at the third sacral vertebra.

At first she'd thought it had just been this guilt which had kept him coming to see her in hospital day after day, and had wished he hadn't felt the obligation. After all, that fateful movie had only been the most casual of dates as far as she'd been concerned—their second evening together, and she'd been planning to break it off gently at that point.

But as time went by, bored, restricted and often in horrible pain, she came to look forward to his visits immensely, to value each gift he brought her and to feel a surge of happiness every time he entered her ward. He would sit for hours, talking, reading, playing games and doing puzzles with her.

It was wonderful of him, she thought. Friendships were stretched and strained by a long hospital stay. No one else gave her the time that Colin did, and her parents were miles away on their farm near Braidwood, and couldn't afford either the time or the money to make the trip to Sydney very often. So slowly, inevitably, fair-haired and wiry Colin became the light of her life and she began to wonder how on earth she would manage without him.

Then it became clear that she wouldn't have to. It was on the day before her discharge that he said to her with deceptive casualness, 'Our names are almost anagrams—have you noticed? Colin and Nicole. As soon as I met you I thought it was an omen, and now. . . Will you marry me? Will we be Colin and Nicole Cotterill, and together for the rest of our lives?'

She agreed out of all sorts of needs that she didn't understand at the time, needs that were to do with the accident and her long confinement and her gratitude. Very wrongly, she thought it was love.

At first it was wonderful. Colin wouldn't let her go back to her parents' to convalesce. 'How will you get proper physiotherapy out there? The drive into Canberra will be way too much for your back! You'll stay here in my flat with me.'

And he looked after her as assiduously as any nurse, leaving her only to go to his job at the bank or to buy groceries and other needs. He arranged his working hours so he could take her to physio, never letting her go anywhere on her own—even when her back improved and she could move without pain.

Never letting her go anywhere on her own. *Never* letting her go anywhere on her own. . .

She would never forget the day she realised that he was locking her into the flat.

'Don't,' she said, trying to be calm and reasonable about it. 'Not until you get a key cut for me. And please do that tomorrow! It gives me the creeps to be shut in!'

He argued, very reasonably, too, about her safety, but there was a flicker of alarm in his eyes and a possessiveness in his arm winding around her back that suddenly made her think, Hang on. . . What's going on here?

Soon it got much worse. He conceded the key, but began to phone her five or even ten times a day from work to ask what she was doing, to check on her plans, and if she didn't answer because she was out on some harmless errand or therapeutic stroll she would hear the phone ringing the moment she re-entered the flat. Then would come his cold, tightly reined anger and his long catechism. 'Where did you go, Nicky? How much did you spend? Who did you talk to? What did they say? Why couldn't you have waited till I got home to go with you, Nicky? I want us to be *together*.'

Then one day her key disappeared again. Lost. Only she knew it wasn't lost at all. Yet even though she was locked in again now the phone kept ringing, and if she didn't answer it or if, God forbid, he got the engaged signal. . . 'Who were you talking to, Nicky?'

She panicked totally inside, although she carefully kept it from showing. He was driving her to her parents' the following weekend and she was terrified that he'd change his mind at the last minute, but he didn't. He was so busy being jealous of non-existent rivals—not just other men, but *anything* in which she expressed an interest that he didn't share—that he didn't notice her inner defection.

Once safely at her parents', she gave him back his ring and told him it was over, and weathered two hours of his unspeakable behaviour—angry rantings, jealous accusations, pleading tears, going on and on about the meaning of their anagramed names—knowing that her father was quietly waiting on the back veranda with his rabbit gun fully loaded.

Now *that* was an over-reaction, she could concede later. Colin had never been violent, had never threatened violence. After finally flinging himself out of her parents' house and gunning his car off their property, however, he went back to Sydney and threw every one of her personal belongings out with the garbage.

This was reported to her by one of her few remaining female friends, and was the last detail needed to convince her to lie low at her parents' for over two months. But she wasn't the sort of person to curtail her life when she'd done nothing wrong. Eventually she gathered up her courage and returned to Sydney to find her pleasant flat, her job with Dr Hill and a new zest for freedom after her year of physical and emotional confinement and pain.

A few months later, needing to know what had happened to Colin, she made careful enquiries from a female acquaintance at his bank and discovered that he was already engaged to someone else—someone who evidently appreciated being 'together' to the point of suffocation.

As for herself, she craved fresh air—literal and metaphorical—with an intensity that she didn't even want to question.

'Let's run. . .let's gallop!' she said restlessly to Richard now. 'I feel like a young horse. The wind's making me frisky.'

She didn't wait for his answer, just grabbed his hand and was off, hearing him laugh just behind her, and they didn't stop till they reached the bridge over the creek, at which point she was breathless and knew she'd been a bit silly because her back was aching, jarred by the pounding rhythm of her feet.

She rubbed at it as they stood at the parapet of the bridge and watched the gurgling tumble of the water, and she hadn't even realised he had noticed until suddenly his hands were there, pressing and massaging as he stood close behind her. He seemed as solid as a wall, close enough for her to feel the light fan of his breathing, and it was all she could do not to sway backwards to rest herself against that sheltering chest.

Somehow, touching her lower spine through layers of clothing, he knew just which muscles to manipulate. After a few minutes he said, 'Better?' It was.

Then he turned her into his arms and they pressed

their cold faces together hungrily. He tasted of the chilly freshness of the late day and his skin was *so* cold against her cheek, but his arms around her were warm and strong and hard. His thighs were locked against hers now, and if she hadn't been wearing gloves she could have thrust her fingers up inside the layered clothing beneath his leather jacket to find out if his back was as muscular as those long hard shapes that pressed against her legs.

'They say food tastes better out of doors,' he murmured against her lips. 'I'd never realised that kisses did, too.'

'Oh, but they definitely do,' she whispered, and they dived together to taste each other once more.

Perhaps he was right. Perhaps 'just sex' might turn out to be the most wonderful thing that had ever happened to her. A whole year of it, if this electricity between them lasted, and then a simple goodbye with no strings attached. . .

It made her wonder suddenly, and she pulled away to say to him, studying the passion-blurred and wind-roughened dark face, 'What about you, Richard? Why aren't you looking for commitment? I know it's a cliché that men don't—that they're purely at the mercy of a woman's nasty little traps—but, in fact, a lot of men are sincere about marriage and all that goes with it. Why not you?'

'Good heavens, the woman wants to discuss this *now*!' he told the big tree just beyond the bridge.

'Yes, now!' she returned. 'You brought it up a few minutes ago, and just because we were kissing. . .'

'Well, exactly! Because we were kissing. Personally, I find the taste of you. . .the feel of you. . .the feel of what you're doing to my— Anyway, I find *that* enough input for my simple brain, but if you need serious conversation at the same time. . .'

'Not at the same time,' she pointed out. 'We've stopped, um—'

'So we have. Pity! But I guess engaging in a searching discussion is one way of putting out this fire until things are a little more private.' He paused, then chose his words carefully. 'I think space is important, Nic. Very important. In any relationship.'

'Yes?'

'Won't that do?'

'A bit brief, don't you think?'

'Simple, rather than merely brief,' he amended. 'It's a statement of faith. Statements of faith should be simple. I think space is important in a relationship.'

'End of subject?'

'Yes.'

'OK,' she conceded, satisfied.

They walked back to his place, not retracing their steps but taking the branch of the bike path that ran up past the library and then turning down the quiet street that led to his. They reached his beige-painted house with its rust-red and forest-green trim just as the last of the light slowly drained from the low, pale sky.

Both of them were starving, and they fought over the Chinese take-out menu for several minutes until they finally arrived at an impossible number of dishes. 'We'll split the left-overs,' he promised her kindly.

'If there are any. I'm pretty hungry.'

'I'm telling you, your eyes are way bigger than that svelte tummy of yours,' he insisted. 'Now, they take a while to deliver so I'm going to jump in the car and pick it up. Want to wait? Or come?'

'Wait,' she answered promptly. 'If you don't mind.'

'Not at all. Just don't read my diary. It's the little pink book with the heart-shaped lock that you can pick with a hairpin.'

She laughed. 'What does a man like you know about those girls' diaries? Not to mention hairpins!'

'Gave one to my eight-year-old niece for her birthday. She loved it.'

'Your niece. . .'

'Lives in Cincinnati, like the rest of my family. Don't worry, I won't be asking you to pass inspection.'

'It hadn't even occurred to me.'

He left and she was alone, forming her own impression of his house in a way she'd been too much on edge to do on Friday. His books—an eclectic assortment that was clearly well loved, with not a medical tome amongst them. His paintings—two, original, both of them dramatic and compelling in this comfortable room with its hardwood floors and 1930s built-in china cabinets. His stereo system—compact yet high-quality, with hundreds of compact discs, running the gamut from rock to classical with excursions into jazz and folk and even country.

It was a comfortable, welcoming, relaxing and well-equipped place to come home to. She wondered, with something stirring inside her, what it was like upstairs. . .

He was back fifteen minutes later, and they both fell upon the food ravenously to the accompaniment, rather incongruously, of Bach. Didn't talk much. Too hungry.

Soon, though, they were utterly stuffed, with at least half of every dish still intact in its container, and he said provocatively, 'I told you so.'

'The portions here are bigger than at home,' she grumbled. 'I didn't realise.'

'Never mind. I'm on call tomorrow night so I can nuke this in five minutes, if necessary, and still get a decent feed. Why don't you take the rice noodles and the shrimp and the rest of the appetisers?'

'Sounds good. Am I. . .going, then?'

They looked at each other across the litter of containers, fortune cookies and paper napkins, and she wished she hadn't said it. It sounded too blunt, too practical. Am I going home now or am I staying and having sex with you?

His mouth had twisted. 'I don't know. Are you? You're welcome—more than welcome—to stay.

Or, if you prefer, you're welcome to go.'

It didn't sound in the least as if he cared one way or the other. She was confused. 'I thought we'd decided. That we were sleeping together. Nothing but, you said.' It sounded awful. Blunt, crude and like a child who wasn't getting the cake it thought it had been promised.

But he laughed, unconcerned. 'And instead we wasted all that time walking and eating? Sorry to disappoint.'

'I didn't mean it like *that*!' She was badly flustered now, horribly embarrassed, and couldn't understand how he seemed so at ease or why he still wanted her when she was being so idiotic.

He had risen now, and was reaching for her hands. She gave them to him, and then he pulled her so that they left the low coffee-table and the untidy remnants of their meal behind and drew her head lightly against his chest.

'My dear Nicole, I would say to you in a moment, "Please stay and grace my bed with your aching loveliness," and I'll still say it if you promise me you're using some form of contraception.' There was a tiny pause. 'Are you?' She felt the tension in his arms as he waited for her answer, which was easy enough to give.

'Actually, I'm not. I'm really sorry.' Timidly, she looked up at him, expecting to see a very male form of impatience and frustration etched in those strong, dark features of his.

But it wasn't there, even though he said, 'I'm incredibly disappointed.'

He *wasn't* disappointed, though, not really, and she couldn't make that out at all. He ought to be, oughtn't he? Men were, she understood, when they expected physical gratification and didn't get it.

'I'm sorry,' she said again, but hardly got the words out before he kissed her, and so thoroughly that there wasn't the possibility of speaking at all.

He was forceful, demanding. If his mouth was trying

to prove something to her then it was succeeding. What was the point in talking, or in worrying over nuances of meaning, when there was this? His fingers fluted along her jawline then swept back to paint her neck with heat. His hands came up into her hair and he groaned, while her own skin tingled and tightened in every pore.

She lifted her face and gave a moan deep in her throat that was almost a groan, and the sound seemed to connect with his own passion and intensify it so that he groaned again too and clutched her—thighs, buttocks, back—with feverish hands.

His house was warm so they'd both taken off the sturdy layers of clothing they'd needed for their walk in the park. Now, he wore just a grey-brown shirt of soft cotton with his jeans, while she wore a silk T-shirt in cinnamon over cream pants in a nubby linen blend. None of these garments offered nearly enough resistance.

When his hand brushed across the silk he might as well have been touching her bare skin. Only when he *did* touch her bare skin seconds later, slipping his hands up beneath the loose blouse to trace the soft swell of her breasts in their lacy bra, the sensation was even more intense and she arched convulsively, wound her arms around his neck and parted her lips to taste him, bite him, moan against his mouth with her eyes closed and her head spinning.

'Let's get something fixed up for you tomorrow, shall we?' Her hands were in his again, and he was rubbing the fine skin on their backs with the balls of his thumbs and pressing his forehead against hers.

'Fixed up? I—' She didn't have a clue what he meant.

'Contraception. Isn't that what we were talking about?'

'That's right. . .' She was still dazed after the intensity of their kiss. 'Let's think. Um. . .'

'I'm an obstetrician, had you forgotten? I do have

access to this sort of stuff, Nic, and a reasonably useful amount of knowledge on such issues as effectiveness and drawbacks.'

'I suppose you do.'

She felt rather foolish, and very *wanton* somehow, discussing it like this—although it would surely have been *more* wanton and incredibly irresponsible not to have discussed it.

With Colin the subject had never come up. He had wanted to wait until they were married, and it hadn't been just because her back had still been very weak that she hadn't made the slightest attempt to change his mind on the issue. The fact that she and Colin hadn't slept together had helped a lot as she emerged from the unhealthy suffocation of that relationship, but now it left her far less experienced than Richard would probably realise.

She had slept with exactly one man four times—well, better than four men one time, she supposed—but she'd been nineteen and not sure, and he'd been twenty-four and on the rebound. Mutually, it hadn't worked. Contraceptively, they'd trusted to luck rather than good management.

Now she was twenty-six and she had seen too many unwanted babies in the course of her work—as, no doubt, had Richard—to be that careless again.

'It's important, isn't it?' she said seriously. 'Let's get it right.'

'We'll talk about it at the office tomorrow when things are quiet.'

'OK.' She lifted her face rather tremulously to find his alert dark eyes regarding her, his expression quizzical.

'I like you, Nic,' he said.

'I like you, too,' she returned immediately, although surely it was a singularly inappropriate exchange at this particular point in their affair.

CHAPTER FIVE

NICOLE was giggling like a schoolgirl and Richard wore an expression which he was desperately trying to pretend wasn't a very silly grin. It was five o'clock, and if anyone else in the practice had known that they were here in his office, going nutty with half a dozen different contraceptive devices amongst a litter of pamphlets pertaining to the said devices, there might have been serious questions asked about Richard Gilbert's suitability for his professional position.

'No, I really don't think I could get into foam or sponges.' Nicole tried to make it sound like a well-considered opinion, but wasn't very convincing. Attempting a trial run of loading the foam into its applicator earlier, she had squirted it all over Richard's desk, and things had gone from there.

'Basically,' Richard attempted to sum up the situation now, 'it should be clear to you at this point that all of these options are really weapons.'

'Well, yes. If ten-year-old boys only knew the great slingshot potential of the—'

'Exactly,' he interrupted firmly. 'Now, obviously, some of these weapons are more lethal than others, and it really comes down to a personal choice.'

'I suppose it does.'

'And it's your call, Nic, as far as I'm concerned.' Suddenly he was very serious. 'I'd never recommend an intrauterine device for a woman who hasn't had children, and I can't see any reason for you to go with the longer-acting implant or injection types but, apart from that, whatever you feel comfortable with. And that includes asking *me* to take the responsibility.'

'N-no, that's all right.'

'Take as much time as you need to make a decision,' he urged, and if he hadn't been an obstetrician she might have found a discrepancy between such a responsible attitude and his stated goal of no-strings-attached sex.

'No, I've decided, I think,' she answered. 'A diaphragm seems best for my needs. *Our* needs,' she amended uncertainly, feeling uncomfortable about the joint pronoun. 'I mean, with the Pill we'd have to wait, wouldn't we?'

'Your salacious impatience is very gratifying,' he drawled, 'and very arousing.'

'Is it? Oh, I didn't mean. . .' She couldn't quite keep the alarm out of her face, but he was suddenly very busy, tidying up the pamphlets and samples, and didn't seem to have noticed.

'In order to preserve a degree of discretion on all sides, however,' he said, 'shall I get you an appointment to have it fitted at Dr Kramer's husband's practice up at St Bart's?'

'Yes, that would be best, wouldn't it?' she agreed.

'Which also means waiting, unfortunately. I doubt Martin Kramer can fit you in before Friday unless I claim special urgency, and that might give a degree of. . .er. . .publicity to this relationship that we wouldn't be happy with, would we?'

We, again. Again, though, she had to agree. 'No. Since it's only a. . .' She hesitated.

'Fling?' he offered helpfully. 'Affair?'

'Yes. I mean, if it was serious. . .'

'Then people could know. But as it is. . .'

'Yes. Much better not to have anyone guess.'

'I'll make an appointment for you, then. Meanwhile. . .'

'Yes?' Somehow it came out a little too eagerly.

'I would suggest a movie. Only there doesn't seem much point, does there?' he finished bluntly with a cool and at the same time openly lascivious grin.

'Not much point at all,' she agreed very decisively, wondering why she felt so giddy that her head was almost spinning.

They spent the rest of the week carefully avoiding contact of any kind, apart from the necessary interchanges over patients. She had her appointment with Martin Kramer first thing on Friday morning, and came away with a prescription for a diaphragm and a strong respect for his impeccably professional attitude. If Beth Kramer's husband had felt the slightest curiosity about why Richard Gilbert himself had arranged this short-notice appointment for one of his nurses he hadn't let it show.

Back at Riverbank Ob/Gyn Dr Gilbert had a full day, with thirty-eight patients to see including an early-morning hysterectomy squeezed into the surgical list for operating room four. His first office patient was already waiting when Nicole arrived, a little late, following her own appointment.

Katie Emerick was sullen and large as she preceded her mother along the corridor to the scales to be weighed.

'I'm sure she'll have put on at least six pounds since her last appointment,' Mrs Emerick said. 'She's eating nothing but junk. I've told her that for the baby—'

'That's not true, Mom,' Katie grumbled, grunting as she got on the scales.

'Six and a half pounds,' Nicole noted.

'See!' accused Mrs Emerick.

'But what does it matter now, Mom? I'm due in four weeks.'

'Babies don't always come when they're due. You might have six more weeks to go, and at the rate you're eating you could put on twenty pounds in that time!'

After sending seventeen-year-old Katie in to produce

her urine sample, Nicole turned to Mrs Emerick and suggested that she wait outside, or perhaps in the examining room if she wanted to be present, but, no, this would not do, apparently.

'Katie doesn't ask the right questions. This whole thing is a disaster! Seventeen, and where's the father? Why couldn't she have taken *precautions*, if she had to behave like a slut. It'll ruin her education, her future. . .'

Katie emerged and said coldly, 'I'm going to manage, Mom. And can you *please* wait outside?'

'No.'

'Yes!'

They glared at each other, a painful battle of wills, and finally Katie won. Which was as it should be at this stage, Nicole considered, as Mrs Emerick stalked, reluctant and angry, back to the waiting room.

She sat the girl down to take her blood pressure, and then asked gently if there were any questions.

'Can Mom not be at the birth?' came the prompt response. 'She's driving me nuts. She says I can't manage on my own, and then she won't even let me try. This is *my* baby and I'm *going* to be a good mother to it! I don't want her there, nagging at me, when I'm in the middle of labour!'

'Then you have the right to say no to her,' Nicole answered. 'I'll make a note of it for Dr Gilbert, shall I?'

'Yes, please.'

Nicole wrote it down in the chart. 'Strong friction between mother and daughter. Katie doesn't want Mom at birth.' Then she ushered Katie into room one and brought the next patient through, wondering how Katie's exam would go.

'See you next week,' she heard several minutes later from Richard. Evidently there were no signs yet, after this first internal examination, that labour was near at hand.

'Meanwhile,' Katie went on, 'I'm going to walk to

school and back every single day for the next four weeks, since you tell me that might help to get it lower.' She smiled, looking the pretty girl that she was, and there was strong determination, too, revealed in the heart-shaped face framed by long ash-brown hair.

So she's staying at school until the very last moment, Nicole thought. That's admirable because it must be embarrassing in her position. I'm not convinced her mother is giving her enough credit. . .

Thirty-six more patients. All of them routine, yet each of them with something unique in their chart or their attitude or their circumstances.

Forty-five-year-old Lesley Dalton was nervous about her scheduled hysterectomy and mourning the end of her child-bearing years. 'Silly, when my youngest is fifteen!' Forty-four-year-old Sharon Gregg's colpos-copy, at which Nicole assisted, decided Richard on recommending a cone biopsy, which was a cautious approach that the patient was happy with.

And forty-three-year-old Jane Morris was glowing in her second trimester and her second marriage. Widowed just a year after her tubal ligation, and with two almost grown-up children, she had married again last year and had had her sterilisation successfully reversed by micro-surgeon, Anne Kennedy.

'You never know what's ahead in life,' she said to Nicole. 'If someone had told me five years ago that I'd be here now, at forty-three, doing *this*, I'd have said I was likelier to be on the moon!'

In the middle of the afternoon Richard snatched a moment to say to Nicole with a frown, 'We haven't actually talked about the weekend.'

'I was assuming we'd—'

'So was I,' he drawled. 'I still am assuming it, only tonight Dr Kramer has conned me into covering her on-call until midnight. Can I reserve you for Saturday?'

'Um, fine. Yes.'

'I'll call you.'

And then Gretchen appeared, needing to borrow Nicole's large blood-pressure cuff, so Richard simply evaporated, it seemed, so quickly did he glide into room three where his next patient was waiting.

Without the prospect of his company, Nicole instead spent the evening joining the Mill Run Athletic Club. Barb had recommended it, and after two weeks here she desperately needed to get back in the pool to keep the strength and flexibility in her back. She swam thirty-two lengths of the twenty-five-metre indoor pool, then ate a light, luscious dinner at the club's café. After a good pause for digestion, she swam another thirty-two lengths and had a long soak in the hot-tub, a bake and steam in the sauna and then a shower and shampoo and blow-dry for good measure.

All of which was, perhaps, why she slept like Rip Van Winkle and didn't make sense of the knocking at the front door the next morning until it was almost too late. Going to the window in the spare room, which overlooked the street, she saw Richard walking towards his car and flew down the stairs to drag the front door open and call him back. She only realised as he mounted the porch steps again that she was wearing just a white cotton lawn nightgown, and one that was semi-transparent with age at that.

'Um. . .I was asleep,' she said creakily.

'I think you're *still* asleep, although perhaps the neighbours across the street *aren't* by now if they've noticed what you're. . .not wearing.'

'Oh. . .' She tried to sweep the full folds of the ankle-length cotton around her to create more layers, but succeeded only in tightening the garment provocatively across her breasts. She was awake enough now—actually, now she was *quite* awake—to see the way his gaze was drawn there as he stepped into the doorway.

'Poor Nicole,' he said softly, brushing his fingers

lightly across the swelling shapes with their crowning
of throbbingly tight pink buds. 'You're cold and still
sleepy. Shall I carry you back to bed?'

'Mmm,' she croaked helplessly. His mouth was very
close to hers now, and his meaning was completely
clear. It filled the scant remaining space between them
like a powerful perfume, making her dizzy with expec-
tation and a slight nervousness that only added to the
sensitivity in every nerve-ending.

A moment later he had lifted her into his arms and
was sweeping her back up the stairs. . .

No commitment. Not a relationship, just a fling.

She certainly had no cause to fear, in the weeks that
followed, that he was becoming too cloying, too possessive. His ideas on where to draw the boundaries in their
affair were very clear and very firm, and he acted on
them with an authority that left her with the relieved
realisation that she didn't need to concern herself with
ambiguity.

They spent an incredibly large proportion of their time
together in bed, and yet she never stayed the whole
night at his place, nor he at hers, which meant that
the expression 'afternoon delight' took on a whole new
meaning for her.

'All this fuss about making love with the light on or
off,' he said to her drowsily one warm Saturday afternoon in late April. 'If people made love in the daytime
more often it wouldn't be an issue. Seeing the way the
sun glows on your body, even on these tiny hairs in the
small of your back—like peach down, only it's even
finer than that—and the way it warms your skin, I want
to knead you like dough. Here, and here, and here.'

She closed her eyes and lay back, aroused by the
knowledge that her body was as familiar to him now as
his was to her. Even that first time had been intense,
wonderful, and not at all the awkward progression she

had feared. From the first he seemed to know just where to touch her, just how to make her breasts swell and her nipples furl, just how to make her hips writhe and shudder, just when to unleash his own unbrookable plunge towards climax so that they hit that tumultuous pinnacle together. . .

When they had this time and were still again, the sun still draping them like a warm, evanescent quilt, she observed idly, tracing the fine stipplings of hair on his forearms with one finger, 'I always thought I'd fancy smooth men, you know, and yet you're anything but.'

'Sorry to disappoint. I'm not offering to shave, either.'

'I should think not! Don't you dare! I actually *meant*—'

'I know what you meant, lovely Nic.'

'No, let me say it,' she begged tenderly. 'I love the hairiness of you. It's so very *male*. Did you know that you can even see this thick patch on your chest through some of your scrubs? Those pale blue ones that you really ought to throw away, they've got so old and thin.'

'And is that a professional or a personal recommendation, Nurse Martin?'

'Professional, of course.'

'Then save it, for heaven's sake!' he growled. 'Till Monday.'

She lay there, quite still, not knowing if he was serious or not and not daring, suddenly, to push the issue. It was one of the things he was rigid about—this separation of their personal and professional lives. And she agreed, of course.

But she'd only been joking just now, a deliberately provocative joke, too, that was much more to do with sex than work. Couldn't he see that? And why was she being so stupid as to get upset about it? It wasn't as if the occasional misunderstanding between them mattered, under the circumstances.

She waited a little longer, with her eyes closed as if

in a state of drowsiness, until the whole thing receded
and seemed too trivial to think about any longer, then
opened her eyes to find him watching her with an
expression she'd seen before—alert, expectant. Or perhaps she was wrong and his look didn't mean those
things at all because whenever she thought she caught it
there he always seemed to have a very practical question
ready for her.

Like now.

'What have you got on for the rest of the weekend?'

Because this was another of their rigid yet unstated
rules. They never spent the whole weekend together,
and if he was on call they didn't see each other at all.

'Believe me, there's nothing that's more of a turn-off,'
he had drawled one day, 'than having your pager go at
a sexually inappropriate moment. And, I promise you,
it's not something you need to experience personally.'

She hadn't argued. Now she said, 'Well, everything's
started growing like mad so I must mow the lawn, and
then I'll swim because otherwise my back might stiffen
up. Barb just has a push-mower. What else? Laundry. . .
Nothing you need to hear about.'

'No,' he agreed firmly at once. 'The domestic details
of someone else's life are unimaginably tedious, don't
you find?'

'Well, not always—'

'*I* do. Spare me your tales of Barb's mower, please!'

'I certainly don't intend to give you a blow-by-blow
account of my battle with the Kentucky blue grass.
Which *isn't* blue, for some reason, despite its name, not
remotely!'

He waved this wail of disillusionment aside. 'Back
to your swimming. Which club is it you've joined?'

'Mill Run. It's the closest and wonderfully luxurious.
Expensive, of course.'

'So I noticed when I joined last week. Hmm. I should
have asked you *before* I joined. I did wonder because I

knew you swam but, as you say, the location and the luxury. . .'

'We can exchange timetable information, if you like, so we don't clash,' she offered, a little tartly.

He really didn't need to create a problem out of it. Would it absolutely matter if by chance they ended up there at the same time every now and then? She never used the gym, and so what if they happened to be churning up and down the pool together? Beneath her state-of-the-art swim goggles he probably wouldn't even recognise her.

'Oh, that's going a bit far, don't you think, Nic?' he drawled, making her *really* annoyed.

'You were the one who thought it might create difficulties,' she retorted, and when he left an hour later, without suggesting dinner, she was entirely undisappointed.

And still angry, to the point where she clacked and clattered around Barb's back yard with the push-mower, then went straight out to Mill Run for her swim, thus leaving a huge hole in Sunday which she refused to consider a problem.

Richard was angry, too.

He was not, however, prepared to fully examine the question of who he was angry *with*. He spent a judiciously timed two hours at Mill Run on Sunday, didn't see Nicole and couldn't help wondering about her back and Barb's mower.

It had been on the tip of his tongue to offer to do it for her yesterday, but he'd wisely managed to restrain that impulse. Mowing someone's lawn for them was definitely approaching a ten on the cosiness scale, and that ought to have been obvious to him the moment she'd mentioned the subject.

As for the issue of their meeting here at the pool, it evidently wasn't going to happen today but, inevitably, it would. Despite his rigorous enforcement of the arcane rules of conduct that were in place between them, he couldn't help smiling at that thought. Nicole in one of those efficient yet still devastatingly attractive—on a figure like hers, at least—racing swimsuits would be quite a sight, and his appreciation of that sight definitely came within the acceptable limits of their current boundaries.

Emphasis on the word 'current'.

There was an enormous amount, however, that was *not* acceptable, it seemed—like the events of Wednesday night.

Nicole drove out to Mill Run straight after work, changed into her practical yet very sleek black swimsuit, showered briefly then chewed up a mile in the pool, cutting through the water like a seal and loving the relentless rhythm of it, the foaming slip of the water on her skin and the healing challenge to her back.

She treated herself to the hot-tub afterwards and her usual lazy use of the hairdryer, which made her pink-gold mane riot and flame. Tonight she folded it carelessly into a French roll, leaving tendrils to fly around her face. Then, very loose in limb and dressed casually in black stretch pants and a black sweatshirt, she got her things and headed out the door.

Or she would have headed out the door, except that the boutique placed strategically right next to it was having a sale and a second swimsuit would come in handy. The sale rack was right at the front, and she was just fingering a conservatively cut green suit and wondering when a dark bulk loomed beside her and a very male voice drawled, 'Definitely not! But how about this?'

Richard.

He lifted a boldly styled navy and white one-piece from the rack and said as he looked at the tag, 'What's your size?'

'In the USA? Six, I think.'

'Snap!'

'No.' She shook her head automatically, unnerved at having him suddenly here like this and even more unnerved by his instant effect on her body, relaxed and sensitised as it was by all that silky-cool water.

'Had you already considered this one?' he persisted.

'No, I— Look at the price, even on sale!'

'Call it a gift, then,' he said softly and teasingly, 'from someone who very much wants to see you in it.'

'No, Richard.'

But he wasn't listening. He'd pulled the swimsuit off the rack and was taking it to the sales desk. He already had his credit card in hand. Nicole's pulses were pounding. She didn't want to make a scene; she didn't want this to be *happening*. . .

It was all done a few minutes later. He handed the carrier bag to her with a grin, saying, 'I look forward to your body's vindication of my taste and judgement. It's going to look stunning on you, I promise.'

And that was when she panicked.

'That's not the point, Richard,' she said, her voice shaky and her hands clutching the suit and its bag convulsively. 'I won't have a man dictating my choice in clothes, buying something for me when I've said no. What gives you that right? To think you know me enough to. . .to *control* me like that? I'm not your doll, to be dressed by you.'

Her voice had begun to rise. In a minute, she realised, people would be staring. Richard already was, those brilliant black eyes of his searching as he struggled to make sense of this. 'Nic?'

A waft of chlorine and carpet cleanser hit her as two wet-haired kids tussled on their way past, and claustrophobia descended.

'I have to go,' she managed, and lunged for the door, not stopping to look back at Richard at all and still unconsciously gripping his unwanted gift in her hands. She raced across the car park, and if he was following her she didn't want to know.

At home, after a badly distracted drive, she slowly began to calm down. *I was an idiot. I was reacting as if he'd been Colin, and there's not a particle of him that's anything like Colin at all. Oh, bloody hell!*

She quickly cooked a packet of fresh pasta and tossed it with a container of pesto sauce then served out a portion, physically hungry after her long swim yet oddly bereft of real appetite. She couldn't finish it. Afterwards, still with her feelings flying around like homeless bats, she went to the bathroom and tried the suit on in front of the long mirror.

It looked great, moulding and containing her figure with its clean lines—the navy contrasting with her bright hair and the white emphasising the creamy smoothness of her skin. It was sturdy enough for serious swimming, yet revealing enough for frivolous fashion.

And it was just a gift, not a mechanism of control. She'd virtually conned Richard into it, too, with her comment about the price, although she hadn't meant it that way. She had overreacted and embarrassed him, quite wrongly twisting his impulsive generosity into something sinister and flinging it back at him in a hysterical torrent of words.

Oh, bloody hell.

He'd probably be home by now. Seizing the impulse before she lost the courage for it, Nicole buttoned herself into a spring coat of dark green leather, put on running shoes with no socks, jumped into the car and drove the two-minute drive to his place.

He *was* home.

'Hi. . .' His greeting at the door was wary. As she entered he added urgently, 'Look, it was an impulse, OK? Not—*hell*! *Not* an act of *control*! Does it really

matter, just this once, that it broke the rules? God,
Nicole—!'

'It was my fault, Richard,' she agreed, her voice taut
with misery. 'Totally my fault. I'm sorry. That's why
I've come. To apologise. And to show you. . .'

She slid the coat off her shoulders and stood there,
wondering if the sockless shoes ruined the effect but
knowing when she saw his gaze that they didn't. . .

'OK.' He sounded a little winded. 'So will you agree
that I've got good taste?'

'If you'll forgive me for ever doubting it and for
doubting your motives.'

He didn't bother to answer, just came to her and slid
the stretchy straps from her shoulders, kissed the tender
hollows above her collar-bones and peeled the suit
slowly, slowly downwards. . .

There was only one problem about her impulsive
swimsuit-modelling excursion—she didn't have any
other clothes. Lying sprawled on top of her in his bed,
Richard told her, 'I've swum half a mile tonight, then
spent half an hour in the gym, not to mention the fact
that there's a certain caloric expenditure involved in. . .
what we do best, and I haven't eaten yet. Have you?'

'A bit. Before. I wasn't hungry.'

'Are you now?'

'Let's just say, do you have any horses available?'

'My housekeeper left a veal stew with rice and green
beans for me to nuke in the microwave. There's plenty
if we pad it out with bread and salad.'

She ate in a pair of his scrubsuit pants and a white
T-shirt, and somehow the outfit must have been more
attractive than she would have imagined because after
the meal—it was getting rather late by this time—he
swept her off to bed again.

She stayed the night—by default, rather than by any
agreement that it would happen.

Lying there in this arms at midnight, tired and happy,

it seemed too difficult to think of getting up, putting on her swimsuit, shoes and coat and going home just yet. In a little while she would do it. She really would. . .

A few moments later they were both asleep, and she didn't waken until the full-bodied sound of classical music swelled suddenly from his clock-radio alarm next morning at half past six.

He was already awake, it seemed, and said immediately, 'Well, will you look at that? There's a strange woman in my bed! And naked, too.'

'Unless we're dreaming,' she answered creakily.

'Do you think we might be?'

'Best to act on that assumption, perhaps.'

'Rather than admit we broke the rules?' he probed.

'Remind me—when did we make that particular rule?'

'I don't think we did, as such,' he said slowly. 'It just seemed. . .obvious. Perhaps it isn't any more.'

He was watching her, and she wasn't at all sure what he wanted. Strenuous denial? She said after a moment, 'I guess. . .last night. . .it was far more convenient for me just to stay. When that's the case perhaps it's silly to make an issue of it.'

'Is it?'

'I'm asking. It's up to you, Richard. We both know we don't want commitment from this, don't want any level of intensity, and since we do both recognise that—'

'We seem to, both of us,' he came in very drily.

'Then why impose an artificial constraint? If you're worried that I'm going to start washing your pyjamas in return for your writing out my bills I promise you I'm not.'

'In fact, that particular worry hadn't occurred to me,' he responded drily, 'although now that you've mentioned it I expect I'll start having hideous nightmares in which you lunge at me with a plastic laundry basket and a bottle of bleach. As for staying the night, I don't

have a problem with it since the underlying parameters
of our relationship are evidently clearly understood and
agreed upon by all parties concerned.'

'OK, then. Good.' She nodded, feeling that she ought
to regard the discussion as a success, although somehow
that wasn't the impression she was left with.

Fifteen minutes later they ate a simple breakfast in
silence.

'My waters broke,' Katie Emerick said.

She was standing in the corridor outside Riverbank
Ob/Gyn's locked office suite at seven-thirty that morning with her school backpack in her hand. There was
something poignant in the contrast she presented—teenage fashion clashing with maternity gear; defiance
clashing with nervous expectancy.

'When?' Richard asked.

'In the bathroom. About an hour ago.'

'Clear?'

'I. . .um. . .'

'The fluid was clear?'

'Oh, yes!'

'You didn't phone, Katie,' Richard accused gently.

'Mom would've heard the call. I just. . .' she hefted
the backpack '. . .pretended I was going to school. What
should I do next?'

'Well, you're a week late,' Richard calculated. He
opened up the office, just as another elevator arrived to
disgorge Cynthia, Darla and Dr Turabian. 'You weren't
dilated or effaced at all at your exam last Friday but
you're young, which often makes things happen fast
once they start. Are you having pains?'

'No. At least. . .like bad menstrual cramps. But that's
not labour, is it? I thought I was supposed to be
screaming.'

'You've been watching too much bad television,
Katie. Nicole?' Richard turned to her. Although they'd

separated at his place immediately after breakfast they'd
still somehow managed to arrive at the hospital together
in their two cars.

'I'll walk her over to Labor and Delivery,' she
answered him, anticipating the request.

'Yes, because I have a thing or two to do here before
rounds. Nicole will help you settle in, Katie, and then
I'll be in to see how you're getting on.'

'This is it, you mean?' Katie said. 'I thought you
might send me home again.'

'This is it, Katie,' he echoed solemnly. She picked
up her backpack, and he added gently, 'How about we
look after that for you in the office, hey?'

Nicole put the heavy, scruffy-looking object away in
a cupboard and then walked Katie to the elevator, down
to the ground floor, through a series of carpeted corridors
and elegantly decorated waiting areas and up again to
the maternity floor.

Katie had two contractions on the way, and she was
no longer dismissing them as 'like menstrual cramps'.
There was something sad about her today, about her
aloneness, despite her obvious intelligence and determination. As they were taken in to a large, pleasant room
overlooking the car park with rapidly leafing out trees
beyond, Nicole began to calculate rapidly.

Richard's first appointment this morning was at nine,
and she had all the patients' charts to get ready. Usually
she liked to prepare pathology slides in advance for
anyone who was having a smear, but she could do it as
she went, like Gretchen did. On the other hand, a nurse
had been assigned to Katie now—Susie, in her early
forties, who seemed nice—and both Katie's labour and
her delivery would take place in this room so she was
in good hands and everything should go smoothly. There
was no real need for her to stay.

Nonetheless, she decided to stay just a bit longer.

Katie used the bathroom and put on a gown, whimpering and tensing through a strong contraction.

'Did you take Lamaze childbirth classes?' Nicole asked her, and the seventeen-year-old shook her head.

'I had enough to do with school. Also, those classes cost money. I wasn't going to ask Mom for it.'

She lay down on the high bed and Susie came in to check her. 'Four centimetres, Katie, that's great. Let's put you on the monitor for a bit, then you can walk around.'

'I think I'd rather stay here.'

'Try it,' Nicole came in. 'It often makes the contractions feel less intense.'

'I think I'd rather rest.'

Unseen by Katie, Susie gave a little shrug. On the monitor the baby's heart rate was good and the contractions showed a good rhythmic progression.

'Why don't you take one little trip around past the nursery?' Susie urged.

'I'll come with you,' Nicole said quickly, and this time Katie agreed.

They took it slowly, passing another woman—an older first-time mother, with her tired-looking husband—as they went. A strong contraction took hold, then they reached the window that looked into the nursery and Katie studied the ten babies there in silence until the next contraction came. It wasn't possible to tell from her expression how she felt about the fact that soon one of the babies in there would be hers.

'I want to go back now,' she said after the contraction had passed, and Richard had just arrived when they reached the room.

Examining her, he pronounced, 'Still four-ish, maybe a little more, and eighty per cent effaced. That's good, Katie. You're doing really well.'

'It's hurting more every time.'

'Susie will help you breathe through it, and that should help. Or would you like an epidural?' He had outlined the various pain relief options to Katie and her mother during a previous office appointment, but nothing had been decided on.

'How much does it cost?' she said now.

'Oh, Katie!' Nicole exclaimed.

But Richard answered seriously, 'You're covered on your mom's insurance, aren't you?'

'Yes, but there's a big co-payment. She'll say something. No, I'll manage without.'

'It seems so sad,' Nicole said to Richard as they walked back up to the Riverbank Ob/Gyn office suite together, 'that she won't take anaesthesia because her mum will object to paying for it.'

'I don't think their relationship is as bad as it sometimes seems,' was his answer. 'Mrs Emerick is just so afraid this will ruin her daughter's future, and fears are sometimes worse in the abstract. Once the baby is actually born. . .'

And, in fact, things started to improve even sooner than that. Shortly before lunchtime Richard took a call from Labor and Delivery in between patients and reported to Nicole, 'Katie's up to eight centimetrès. And her mom is there. An hour ago Katie asked Susie to phone her, and apparently she's handling the contractions much better now that Mrs Emerick is encouraging her through them. Let's try to squeeze these last four patients in as quickly as we can. All Ob checks?'

'Three Ob checks, one annual.'

'Sounds do-able. With any luck Katie will deliver over lunch and not throw off anyone's schedule.'

It wasn't quite as straightforward as this, however.

One of the Ob checks was for Kathy Solway, a bright, committed woman of about Nicole's own age, who was still clearly very much a newlywed. Nicole had liked her when they'd first met on her previous visit. At eighteen weeks of pregnancy she had had blood drawn for her alpha-fetoprotein screening, a test which could indicate neural tube defects if the particular level in the mother's blood was high, or Down's syndrome if it was low.

While not as reliable as amniocentesis or chorionic villus sampling, the test posed no risk to the foetus and was usually performed routinely in this practice between the sixteenth and eighteenth weeks.

Kathy had read the information about the test carefully and had decided to go ahead with it, saying sensibly, 'If it does show the possibility of a problem I can go on to have a more accurate test, can't I? And if it's normal I'll stop worrying.'

'Have you been worrying?' Nicole had asked.

Kathy had smiled. 'Not really. I'm young, and there's no family history of major problems. I've been careful about my diet and lifestyle, too, even before I was pregnant. Mike says he had no idea he was marrying such a saint!' She had blushed a little.

And the afp screening had been normal. On that visit, too, Nicole had given Kathy a very sickly-sweet carbonated drink to take home with her and, as instructed, she had dutifully drunk it forty-five minutes before her appointment today so that blood could be drawn and tested for abnormal sugar. Again, this was a somewhat crude indicator, but an easy test that posed no risk to the foetus and one that could then be followed up more thoroughly if there was a positive result—this time for any signs of gestational diabetes.

'Not that I'm worried about *that*, either,' Kathy said as she went in to have her blood drawn by Nurse Ellen Glover, whose job it was today.

'Any other questions or concerns before I send you in to see Dr Gilbert?' Nicole asked routinely after she'd taken blood pressure and pulse.

'Well, not really,' Kathy answered. 'Although. . .' She hesitated and frowned. 'I have been having a lot of those Braxton-Hicks contractions yesterday and today. Is that normal at this stage?'

Nicole concealed her alarm and said carefully, 'It can be. Tell me more about them. Are they painful?'

'Just a bit. Like mild menstrual cramps. They seem to last about half a minute.'

'Regular? Or not?'

'Well, sort of. I mean, they'll come every ten minutes for a while and then stop.' She had sensed Nicole's concern now. 'You don't think. . . It's not labour, is it?'

'Um, probably not,' Nicole answered, though she felt she might be overstating the case. Kathy's blue eyes had widened in alarm and her breathing had quickened. 'I'm going to tell Dr Gilbert what you've said, though. He may want to do a pelvic exam. Do try and describe the contractions to him as best you can, and think about any other symptoms.'

'Other symptoms. . . Well, there has been some discharge, not bloody. More like—' She broke off. 'No! It's too soon! I'm only twenty-two weeks. The baby couldn't survive!'

'Please don't worry,' Nicole reassured her. 'Even if it is preterm labour we've caught it in plenty of time and Dr Gilbert should be able to stop it. Come in to the examination room now and take off your lower clothing so he can check your cervix. We'll soon know.'

Kathy went in, flustered and upset. 'Mike told me to call last night but I was so sure it was Braxton-Hicks and nothing to worry about. I've been doing everything right!'

'This *isn't* your fault, Kathy,' Nicole told her urgently.

Richard emerged from room three just after she had closed the door of room two behind Kathy and she spoke to him quickly. 'You're due to see Mrs Hudson in room one next, but can you take room two instead? It's Kathy Solway, and I've upset her, I'm afraid, by suggesting—' She outlined the situation and he nodded, frowning.

'Discharge? If she means part of her mucous plug. . .'

He disappeared into room two and came out several minutes later to report, 'Yes, she's started to efface, and she's dilated to a finger-width. Hasn't had any contractions for the past hour, but had one just as I finished the exam. I'm going to send her home on bed-rest and see if that will do it. But first we'll try a sonogram to see if there's any obvious cause.'

There wasn't, and a concerned Kathy was driven home by her husband, whom she had phoned to come in for her. Richard was confident of the outcome at this stage, however. 'She's the kind of patient who'll take her bed-rest seriously, which makes my job a lot easier.'

The schedule had got out of kilter, though, of course, and the last two patients encroached some minutes into Richard's lunch-hour. Then, before he could escape to the hospital cafeteria, Labor and Delivery paged him to say that Katie Emerick was ready to deliver. 'Which, if all goes well, will put our afternoon back on track, and it will only be my stomach that suffers,' Richard said.

All did go well, and Richard was able to report as he bolted a freshly delivered pizza, 'A girl. Alicia Catherine. Nice size. Katie lost control a bit at the end, but those contractions had got pretty intense. Now she's beaming, and so is her mom. The thing I *hate*, though. . .' his face suddenly darkened '. . .is the fact that her insurance limits her to a twenty-four-hour hospital stay.'

'The mothers hate it, too,' Nicole came in. '*And* the nurses!'

'Those sorts of dictates are going to backfire in a big way, with more post-partum problems going undiagnosed until they turn into something serious. Fewer mothers are confident enough to stick with breastfeeding—and we're finding more and more areas all the time in which bottle-feeding simply *isn't* as good.

There's a whole host of problems that bottle-fed children are more prone to.'

'Yes. Ear infections?'

'Even the odds of getting juvenile-onset diabetes—aside from the fact that it's inhuman to send a woman home a bare forty-eight hours or even less after a C-section.' He used the common American shorthand for Caesarean deliveries. 'I'm convinced it'll cost the insurance companies *more* in the long run.'

He rasped an angry sigh. 'Well, we'll have Stephanie or Missy call her tomorrow afternoon and again on Monday to see if she's got any concerns or questions. Totally inadequate as follow-up but that's the system, and we can only offer that because this practice is prepared to employ two full-time nurses purely for phone consultations.'

He disappeared, still grumbling, into his office, the pizza being demolished with unnecessary violence. Nicole found herself trying to think of ways to improve his mood—ways which were not entirely forbidden due to the mutually agreed-upon nature of the contract between them. After ten minutes—in which she dismissed flowers delivered with a romantic note, an illicit kiss in the ultrasound room and half a dozen other possibilities—she decided there was nothing. Absolutely nothing she could do that wouldn't earn her a terse comment about 'breaking the rules'.

Like Katie being too scared of her mother's response to ask for an epidural, it suddenly seemed a little sad.

CHAPTER SIX

WITH May came the advent of reliable warm weather in central Ohio, and the full leafing-out of trees and shrubs. Garden fever suddenly took hold, and everyone rushed to the plant nurseries to acquire flats of impatiens, petunias and marigolds and fling them into the annual beds that bordered their lush lawns. Northmoor came into its own as a truly beautiful place to live.

Nicole soon felt obliged to follow the gardening trend for the sake of Barb's property value and relationship with the neighbours—not to mention the fact that it was very satisfying to create such a riot of wonderful colour—but her back forced her to take it slowly so her weekends in May were pretty full.

Richard didn't offer to help. And why should he? She wouldn't have *wanted* it, actually, and he'd been scathing on the subject of shared domesticity quite often enough for her to be in no doubt as to his feelings on the subject. If it bothered him that her weekends were so taken up with all this labour, as well as her necessary swimming and an outing or two with Gretchen or another nurse from the practice—which added up to mean that they didn't get to spend much time together— then that was *his* problem.

And of course one weekend in four he was on call, and he was still quite firm about the fact that on such weekends she should stay away. Which was all quite fine with her!

Then came June and it was undeniably summer, and she could put the garden in a holding pattern and think of other things—like the fact that she wanted to explore the environs of Columbus more extensively and do some actual hiking. It was a bit embarrassing that she knew more about Richard Gilbert's body than about the parks and state forests around central Ohio, and that her chief pedestrian exercise consisted of walking the three blocks to his house or, on a good day, strolling with him through Northmoor Park to look at the Olentangy River.

She had been noticing lately, too, that the necessary avoidance of Richard's name outside the context of work in her letters to her parents was making it hard to think of an adequate quantity of news.

She made the mistake, however, of telling Richard that she wanted to see more of the region, and unfortunately he took it as a hint and drew up an itinerary then and there.

Which was why they were here, now, in his car at half past ten on a sunny but not too humid June Sunday morning, driving east from Columbus to visit and picnic at the Dawes Arboretum.

The road was pretty enough but rather straight and flat, and Richard was obviously tired of being at the wheel when he said to her just after New Albany, 'Entertain me, Nic. I'm bored with the society of my own thoughts. I want yours.'

She laughed. He had a nice way with words sometimes—light and elegant, like a chocolate soufflé. She told him this, and he laughed, too.

'I always perform better with the right audience.'

'And is that what you want me to do now?' she asked. 'Perform?'

'Yes, please.'

'I don't think my thoughts contain the right raw material for anything very scintillating.'

'Did I ask for scintillating?'

'You asked to be entertained.'

'Yes, but, you know, in art it's not the content it's

"PINBALL WIZ"

Scratch the gold circles and claim up to

**4 FREE Books
and a FREE Gift!**

See inside

NO RISK, NO OBLIGATION TO BUY... NOW OR EVER!

How to play "PINBALL WIZ" and be eligible to receive up to FIVE FREE GIFTS!...

1. With a coin, carefully scratch away the gold circles opposite. Then, including the numbers on the front of this card, count up your total pinball score and check the conversion table to see how many FREE books and gifts you are eligible to receive.

2. Send back this card and you'll receive specially selected Mills & Boon® novels from the Medical Romance™ series. These books are yours to keep absolutely FREE.

3. There's no catch. You're under no obligation to buy anything. We charge you nothing for your first shipment. And you don't have to make a minimum number of purchases - not even one!

4. The fact is, thousands of readers enjoy receiving books by mail from the Reader Service™. They like the convenience of home delivery and they like getting the best new romance novels at least a month before they are available in the shops. And of course, postage and packing is completely FREE!

5. We hope that after receiving your free books you'll want to remain a subscriber. But the choice is yours - to continue or cancel, anytime at all! So why not accept our no-risk invitation. You'll be glad you did!

A SPECIAL GIFT FOR YOU IF YOU SCORE OVER 51 POINTS!

You'll look a million dollars when you wear this lovely necklace! Its cobra-link chain is a generous 18" long, and the lustrous simulated pearl completes this attractive gift.

NOT ACTUAL SIZE

Play
"PINBALL WIZ"

▶ Up to 4 free Medical Romance™ novels
▶ A free simulated pearl necklace

PINBALL WIZ POINTS CONVERSION TABLE	
Score 51 or more	**WORTH 4 FREE BOOKS** PLUS A SIMULATED PEARL NECKLACE
Score 41 to 50	**WORTH 4 FREE BOOKS**
Score 31 to 40	**WORTH 3 FREE BOOKS**
Score 30 or under	**WORTH 2 FREE BOOKS**

YES! I have scratched off the gold circles. Please send me all the gifts for which I qualify. I understand that I am under no obligation to purchase any books, as explained on the opposite page. I am over 18 years of age.

M8BI

MS/MRS/MISS/MR   INITIALS

BLOCK CAPITALS PLEASE

SURNAME

ADDRESS

POSTCODE

◀ DETACH AND RETURN THIS CARD TODAY. NO STAMP NEEDED! ▶

THE READER SERVICE : HERE'S HOW IT WORKS

Accepting the free books and gift places you under no obligation to buy anything. You may keep the books and gift and return the despatch note marked "cancel". If we don't hear from you, about a month later we will send you 4 brand new books and invoice you for just £2.20* each. That's the complete price - there is no extra charge for postage and packing. You may cancel at any time, otherwise every month we'll send you 4 more books, which you may either purchase or return - the choice is yours.

THE READER SERVICE™
FREEPOST SEA3794
CROYDON,
Surrey
CR9 3AQ

2

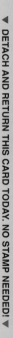

▼ DETACH AND RETURN THIS CARD TODAY. NO STAMP NEEDED! ▼

the execution,' he explained earnestly. 'Think of a still life. It might be just a bowl of fruit and a jug, but in the hands of the right artist. . .'

'So the fact that I was actually thinking, when you first asked, about how different the sheep look here. . .'

'Different how?'

'Bigger, with longer legs and less wool, like some weird breed of dog. They're definitely not merinos.'

'There you are, you see, that's interesting. What makes you an authority on sheep breeds?'

'My parents are farmers. Hadn't I told you?'

'Nic, we haven't told each other much, you know,' he pointed out gently. 'We tend to spend a lot more time. . .doing other things.'

'Yes,' she had to agree. It came out a little faintly. 'I suppose we do. . .'

Today, though, they did talk—about farming and life in Australia—for the rest of the drive, ending with the sparkle of tears in Nicole's eyes and the admission, 'Silly! I've made myself homesick now!' Over lunch, eaten at the edge of the roofed picnic shed at the Arboretum, they talked about which trail they would take first after lunch to explore this lovely place.

They had both contributed to the picnic. She had made huge ham and salad sandwiches on French bread, while he had brought carbonated juice and mineral water, a delectable berry fruit salad, chocolate chip cookies and a Thermos of tea. 'Since I've noticed what you're like at the office if you don't get your lunchtime cup,' he commented.

And such was the relaxed atmosphere, with other tables of picnickers close by and a gorgeous backdrop of lush, summery trees, that the forbidden reference to their working lives during leisure time passed without comment on both sides.

After the picnic had been completely demolished and tidily packed away, they took the trail that they'd decided on. It led down through fragrant pine forest to a Japanese garden with formal raked gravel, a mossy-roofed shelter, a large koi-filled pond and ornamental bridges.

Beyond the Japanese garden came a sunny slope, planted with dozens of species of holly, then a cool lush forest of deciduous trees which opened into a glade filled by a pioneer family graveyard, so old now that it had ceased to convey the aura of death and contained only beauty and a rather poignant sense of history.

They wandered around it together for quite some time, pointing out the inscriptions on the simple, worn old stones and creating stories together out of the sparse details given—long lives and short ones, success and failure, marriage and children, happiness and loneliness.

'Just out of interest, Nic. . .'

'Mmm?'

'Are you afraid of loneliness?'

'You mean. . .?' She looked up at him. They were standing in front of one of the oldest graves, with the afternoon sun warming their backs and no one else here for the moment. His dark face was intent, yet the corners of his firm mouth were lifted in the slightest of smiles. 'In what context?'

'In a long-term sense. I mean. . .' He chose his words carefully. 'There are those who would say that that's what you. . .*we*. . . are setting ourselves up for in life by rejecting the notion of a lifelong exclusive commitment to one person, symbolised by marriage.'

'I never said I rejected that notion, Richard.'

'Ah,' he responded. 'Didn't you? Forgive me, I thought that was the whole premise upon which this relationship was based.'

'Yes.' She pounced, feeling clever. '*This* relationship.'

'But not the next one?'

'Don't paint me into a corner!' she returned, flustered

now by his sharp probes and no longer feeling clever at all. 'Don't spoil this! I—I'm not thinking that far ahead, OK? Maybe one day. . .but, no, don't make me try to guess how I'll feel five years in the future.'

'Five years?'

'I don't know! All I know is what I need now, and since it's what you want too, as you've stated quite clearly time after time, don't borrow trouble. Aren't *you* afraid of loneliness?'

But she should have known that turning his own question back on him would be a mistake.

'To quote you, Nic,' he answered lightly at once, 'I'm not thinking that far ahead.'

He gave a maddeningly complex and unreadable smile and wandered off to the next grassy grave, apparently quite satisfied with the conversation. Nicole could not feel the same. He *did* this to her! Probing at her and then refusing to reveal as much as she had. She always got the feeling that he thought he'd learned more from what she had said than she was aware of having revealed, and hated the fact that some of their discussions thereby took on the aura of fencing matches, with feint and parry, cut and thrust.

'You *bug* me, Richard Gilbert,' she told him now. 'You really get under my skin!'

And he actually laughed, the maddening, horrible man.

They left the graveyard and followed the trail to an old log cabin, with its little cool-house built over the nearby creek, then came back up the hill and out into the open by the picnic shelter and the car park once again.

'Oops,' he said. 'Hadn't realised we were going to lose our cover so quickly.'

'Wh—?'

But he'd already coaxed her back into the trees, glanced back along the trail to see that no one was

coming and then pulled her with one elegantly fluid
movement into his arms.

'Haven't kissed you all day,' he muttered. 'And that's
way beyond the limits of my endurance.'

His kiss was rough and hungry and satisfying, making
her forget how irritated she'd been. It was a different
kiss, somehow. Tasting him and melting into every
familiar contour of his body as she held him and ran
gloating hands over his back and his shoulders and the
two rounded knots of a very sexy male behind, she
couldn't work it out at first.

More urgent? No, not that. All of their kisses were
urgent—except when recent satisfaction made them
very lazy. More demanding? Again, no. There was no
need for him to make demands. She gave him everything
quite willingly.

Then she realised what it was—he was happy. The
tension in his muscles was elastic and exuberant, he was
smiling as he kissed her and when he lifted her off
the ground to kiss her some more it seemed effortless
for him.

This was all very nice for *him*! She had to admit to
herself, though, that she wasn't feeling the same and
didn't in the least understand why *he* was. Fighting her
feet back to solid ground, she—reluctantly—pulled her
mouth from his, took his rough male jaw between
her palms and studied his face, frowning.

'So, is it the glorious beauty of nature?' she
demanded.

'Is what?' he returned.

'That's responsible for this sudden inrush of *joie de
vivre*. You're kind of *glowing*, Richard.'

He shrugged. 'Nothing, really.'

'Don't be difficult.'

'OK,' he conceded. 'Just you, Nic. You've been. . .
making me happy lately. Nice. Simple. Happy. I like it.'

'Even when I'm mad at you?'

'But you're not really, are you?'

'Yes! When you confuse me like this!'

'Oh, I'm confusing you? Surely not! How?' He was grinning in an evil way.

'Oh, I don't know,' she said crossly. 'By saying one thing when you seem to be feeling another. I feel you're *playing* with me sometimes. *Toying* with me.'

'Never, Nic,' he answered, suddenly serious. 'Playing with you, maybe. In the nicest possible way. Toying with you? Never! Believe that, OK?'

'If you say so.'

'Trust me.'

'I *don't*, you know! I absolutely don't!'

He refused to be cowed by her threatening tone and took her hand, saying, 'Come on. Let's see the rest.'

She thought about pushing the issue, but the feel of his hand enclosing hers was so nice, as was the confident, rhythmic crunch of his footsteps in time with hers. . . Weakly she let it all slide and bartered away the possibility of understanding him better for the sake of this vivid but momentary physical pleasure, refusing to look at the fact that at some point in the future she might regret that choice.

They didn't leave the arboretum until nearly five, then stopped impulsively on the way home for a spicy Mexican dinner at a large, noisy restaurant. He had a Mexican beer, she drank a tangy margarita cocktail and they ate a creamy green chili soup topped with corn chips, followed by beef and chicken fajitas garnished with guacamole, salsa, refried beans, grated cheese and salad. Then, thirsty from the savoury spices, she had another margarita.

It was a mistake. They were stronger than they tasted. He hadn't ordered a second beer, and she asked him a little lightheadedly, 'Not thirsty?'

'On call after nine,' he reminded her.

'Oh. That's right. I'd forgotten.' She felt a sudden,

plunging disappointment, and the next thing she said
was definitely the fault of the drink. 'That means I can't
stay all night. R-rats!'

'It's only seven,' he pointed out gently. 'We can
still. . .'

'I know, but. . .' It was still the drink. 'I like *staying*.
Cuddling you. Hearing you *snore*.'

'Which I have never done in my life,' he came in
indignantly at once, and she saw—woozily—an irresist-
ible opportunity to tease.

'Not as long as you're on your side,' she conceded
seriously. 'I have to r-roll you sometimes, then
you stop.'

'Do you really roll me, darling?'

'Yes. You're a sound sleeper. And you're heavy.
Lovely and warm, though. And I don't mind having to
roll you off your back because then I can wrap my arms
ar-around you from behind.' It *had* to be the drink. 'And
you feel so good. And you don't snore any more.'

'Actually, I still refuse to believe that I *ever* snore.'

'Well, if you prefer to think s-so,' she told him kindly.
'Anyway, even when you do I love it, only tonight I'll
have to—.'

'Stay. Please stay!'

'But you've always said—'

'Sometimes exceptions have to be made. Like when,
as a doctor, I judge that you're a little too tipsy to be
quite safe alone in your own house.'

'Oh.'

'Teasing. Just teasing. Please stay. . .'

'OK.'

So they drove to his place and she stayed, and he was
called out at two to deliver Jane Morris's baby, although
Nicole was sleeping off the effects of those two margar-
itas too thoroughly to even stir as he quickly switched
off his beeper, called the hospital, dressed and left the

house. Things were going fast, according to the labor and delivery staff.

Too fast. With her two almost-grown children from her first marriage, Jane had the confidence of a veteran and the slightly fuzzy and too rosy memory of someone who hadn't done this for a while. She'd left it a little late to come in, she was three week early and the baby wasn't big enough to take its time getting through the birth canal. Although the drive over the river took three minutes at most at this time of night, she was already panting urgently when Richard arrived and they'd called the Ob resident on call in case he didn't make it.

Three strong pushes in five minutes and she'd delivered a perfect little boy. At forty-eight, it was Dan Morris's first child and he was emotional and over the moon, giving Richard such a twist of envy in his gut for a minute that he couldn't steady his hand enough to start repairing the small tear Jane had sustained in her perineum.

Then this suddenly became of secondary importance as she began to bleed badly, and it took a good hour to pack the uterus, inject the right drugs, step up the IV infusion and bring things under control.

'That's right,' Jane said finally and vaguely, still weak and trembling and happy, not realising quite what a close call it had been. 'This happened with Colleen and Corey, too. Maybe not as much bleeding. . .'

'Mrs Morris, you didn't tell us that,' Richard pointed out patiently.

'I'd forgotten. It was so long ago. I thought I had it all under control. I guess, Dan, I've been showing off a bit, haven't I? Because it's your first but not mine. How horrible! I—I won't any more. From now on, it's all new for both of us.'

'It *is* new, too,' said the nurse, Jennie, very firmly. 'Every one of them, is different from the word go, and it's dangerous to forget it!'

Veteran of six births of her own and sixteen years in Riverbank's Labor and Delivery, she knew what she was talking about.

'When do we see him again?' Dan Morris asked gruffly.

'Matthew, he means,' Jane said.

'We know who he means, honey,' Jennie assured her. 'Matthew's safe in the nursery, and you'll see him as soon as you're moved to your room.'

Richard made the belated repair to the perineum and then left, sporting numerous artistic blood splatters all over his green scrubs. It was a happy outcome, though, and he thought again of what Jane had said several times during her prenatal office visits. 'Little did I think five years ago that at forty-three I'd be doing *this*!'

Nicole had mentioned five years today, too. Lives changed. People changed. More than they themselves could ever predict. He smiled suddenly at the wheel of his car, and felt his loins stir at the thought of being beside her again minutes from now.

She was in the midst of a nightmare. He had crept up the stairs and slipped into the bathroom for a brief shower, towelled himself then gone naked into the room, wondering with a very male sense of need if she would respond to being gently awoken with love-making. But she was thrashing about and muttering torn snatches of words.

'No, Colin!' he heard, and the male name shocked him horribly. 'Colin. . . The baby. . . The postman's coming. . . Let me out. . . Ah!'

This last cry woke her. She was panting and had flung herself back against the pillows, her hair in a tangled pink-gold shimmer across the pale fabric and her eyes wide, as he slid onto the bed beside her.

'It's OK, Nic. It's OK. . .'

Nicole fought him off at first, her mind still tangled in the web of her ugly dream. Was it Mexican food?

She'd been locked in Colin's flat, and the postman was coming to deliver a baby and she had to help him. If she didn't he would just leave the baby, newborn and naked, on the ground beside the letter-box, like a parcel, because it was too big to fit in. So Colin had to let her out, but he wouldn't.

He kept saying that he couldn't because she didn't really care about the baby. Only she did, and she kept telling him so but he wouldn't listen, wouldn't believe her, and then it was too late because the postman had dropped the baby—

'Nic. . . Nicole. . .' Whose was that soothing voice?

'Oh, Richard!' she breathed.

'It was just a dream, Nic.'

'I—I know.'

'Do you want to tell me about it?'

'I don't think so. It's fading now. You know, dreams never make any sense.'

'You said someone's name.' He cleared his throat and then cleared it again, impatiently. 'Colin.'

'Oh. Yes. The man I was engaged to. I dreamt that he'd. . .locked me in and I wanted to get out.' She laughed briefly. 'It was silly, actually. I had to get out to deliver a baby. Is that where you were?'

'Yes.'

'I guess subconsciously I must have noticed you go. . .'

'I guess. . .'

'How was it?'

'A boy for Jane Morris but, shh, get back to sleep. You don't need details at this hour.'

He slid closer and put an arm around her, then pulled the sheet up over them both. It was a warm night and they didn't need anything heavier. She felt the vivid presence of the nightmare ebbing away and seized onto this far happier reality, nourished by the detail of it, in contrast to the vague, looming terrors of the dream. His hair was slightly damp at the ends, he smelled clean from top to toe, and—

And, she suddenly realised, he was naked.

And aroused. It was fairly quickly contagious, and yet—with both of them tired and the whole world, it seemed, so sleepy and dark—the whole thing was incredibly slow and lazy. Soft, lazy kisses, warm drowsy hands at her breasts, a gentle fitting together of their two bodies and a shared climax that just swelled between them like the rolling muscle of an unbroken wave. When it ebbed they were both asleep, still locked together, within seconds.

Elaine Bridgman was taking the first appointment that morning. Now at almost thirty-five weeks of pregnancy, she was still working part time in the billing office, although she tended to spend more hours there than she was paid for.

'I feel safer being on hand with up to five obstetricians and several nurses within earshot,' was her explanation, 'since Dr Gilbert isn't confident that I'll be able to tell when I'm in labour.'

The latter was taking a very safe approach to the pregnancy at this stage. 'I could have you admitted,' he had told Elaine several weeks ago, 'but there's really no call for it if you're careful. What I do want to do is make sure you're extra alert for any other signs of labour.'

'Like my waters breaking?'

'Well, that's generally fairly obvious, and happens quite late in labour for many women. But there are other things. Losing your mucous plug can be an early warning sign. You can feel the tightening of your abdomen in a contraction by resting your fingertips lightly there.'

He was starting weekly internal examinations slightly earlier than usual, and the first of these was today. As always, Paul Bridgman had accompanied his wife, and showed his underlying anxiety as soon as she was out of earshot.

'Every week I tell myself, well, we've got this far, but it's labour that worries me now,' he told Nicole.

'Dr Gilbert is very confident that things will be fine, you know.'

'I know. . .'

'Are you able to take time off work after the birth?' Nicole asked him.

'Just a week. In that area, though, we have things well organised. Elaine's sister has a ten-month-old, and they're going to team up with their child care at our place. Marybeth will handle anything that requires a lot of mobility, while Elaine will be able to manage all sorts of stuff on her own.'

As at previous appointments Elaine's blood pressure, weight, glucose and protein levels were all just as they should be, and after her internal Richard reported cheerfully to Nicole, 'Nothing yet. Cervix is thick and closed. With her lesion just above the T6 level, she may have some dysreflexia when labour begins and I've warned her about that.'

'Does she ever have it normally?' Nicole knew he was referring to the sudden onset of high blood pressure which was often experienced by certain people with spinal cord injuries, triggered by something as slight as a full bladder but disappearing as soon as the trigger was removed.

'Occasionally. Like a lot of people, she knows it as "quad sweats" and has never worried about it much but in labour she may need an epidural to bring it under control. Aside from that, I really don't have any concerns about the whole thing. Next patient ready?'

'Yes,' Nicole said, switching her focus. 'And guess what? I think she's in labour. She hasn't said anything, but she certainly looks uncomfortable and she was due last Thursday.'

'Let's see. . . Robyn Adams? It's her first. Perhaps she's not sure. Hang on, Elaine's still around, isn't she? And Paul? Could you call them back?'

'Sure. . .' She looked a question.

'Robyn's a good sport. If they *are* contractions, and she doesn't object, I'd like Elaine and Paul to have a good look and a feel so that they'll be sure to recognise that distinctive hardening of the uterus.'

He ducked quickly into room four, to emerge a few minutes later. 'Two minutes apart. She thought it couldn't be labour because they started off like that with no gradual increase in frequency. I'll check her cervix now, but do call the Bridgmans back because, despite the two-minute thing, I somehow suspect she's not that far along.'

Nicole went quickly down to the front office, where Paul was saying to his wife, 'Yes, I got the casserole out of the freezer. So I'll pick you up at five?'

She explained what Richard wanted to show them, and they were happy to have the chance to see it first hand. As Richard had predicted, too, Robyn didn't object.

'Except that I can't *believe* I'm only two centimetres,' she said. 'This has been going on for three hours.'

'And you didn't think it was labour?' Richard teased gently. 'What *did* you think it was?'

'Oh, you know, an extra-long cluster of Braxton-Hicks or something. You *said* they'd start at forty-five minutes to half an hour apart, Dr Gilbert! And that's what all the books say, too.'

'The books and I also say that every woman is different,' he answered.

'Well, I didn't think that *I* would be,' she grumbled cheerfully, lifting her head from the examining table. 'With everything else in this pregnancy, I've been so normal they could have written the textbook about me. Yikes, here it comes again. . .'

Her swollen abdomen heaped up visibly into a tense, rock-hard ball and she breathed through the pain rather frantically.

'Gee, you really can see it!' Paul murmured.

'Try feeling it, too, when the next one comes,' Richard suggested.

'Um, if it's OK with. . .'

'Oh, go ahead!' Again Robyn was quite cheerful. 'I expect I'll have half a dozen different nurses doing far worse to me before the day is out.'

They waited, and when the contraction came Elaine splayed her fingers and laid them gently on Robyn's abdomen. 'Yes,' she said. 'Yes, I can feel it quite distinctly. Try it, Paul.'

He did, after another apology to the nicely tanned tummy in question, then nodded, too.

'Sometimes the baby's movements can feel that way towards the end, but it won't have the rhythmic build and ebb,' Richard said. 'Thanks, Robyn. Now, did you drive here?'

She made a face. 'Yes. Was I bad?'

'Very bad. Let's have Nicole call your husband and we'll get you along to Labor and Delivery. Unless you'd like to go home for a couple of hours.'

'Home?' she wailed. 'Won't I have a baby in a couple of hours?'

'Probably a bit longer than that. You don't *have* to go home but I know you're close to the hospital.'

'Think I'll feel safer in the hospital. Just in case,' she added with bright optimism, 'it gets going really fast.'

It didn't. A routine morning passed and, after checking on Robyn Adams just before lunch, Richard reported, 'Up to four centimetres. Her husband's there, and she's going to have an epidural because she's not getting much of a break. The baby's still sky-high, too.

Dr Mason will deliver her late tonight, I expect, since he's on call.'

That afternoon, Katie Emerick came in for her six-week post-partum check, which brought Nicole up short. Was it really six weeks since that morning they'd found her standing in the corridor in the early morning quiet? Yes, in fact it was a little more than that.

Which meant it was six weeks since she'd first stayed the night at Richard's. The thought of time drifting by like that churned her up for some reason, but she didn't have time to analyse the problem now.

Katie looked young and tired and happy, and baby Alicia was blossoming. But it was Mrs Emerick who showed the biggest change. 'She's smiling already. She's just a *love*, aren't you, Alicia? And Katie did so well in her exams. She's going to college in the fall, and I was so sure it just wouldn't work out. No, Katie, you go in by yourself. I'll sit out here and hold the baby, if I'm not distracting Nurse Nicole.'

'Not at all,' the latter answered.

She took the next patient's weight, specimen and blood pressure, then ushered her into room two and snatched a moment to chat with Carol Emerick. Alicia really was gorgeous. She said so. 'And what is Katie planning to study?'

'She's going to take pre-med courses, here at Ohio State. I can't believe it! Katie a doctor one day! She's so determined! I own a quilting store and she's working there for me over the summer. This was all her idea. She's living at home, *not* for the free baby-sitting—as I'd feared—but so that she can help and "earn babysitting credits", as she puts it, which she'll reclaim when college starts and I take Alicia during her classes.

'Same with the hours she puts in at the store. We should be able to manage it that way for the whole first year, and then. . .well, we'll have to see. There's a nice pre-school and day-care centre right near my store. I don't mind helping Katie when she's doing so much to help herself.'

'He says my cervix is incredibly healthy,' Katie reported when she emerged, then she whispered to Alicia, 'I wonder what on earth *that* means!'

'We'll send you a card a year from now to remind you of your annual pap,' Nicole told her.

'And that's it?'

'That's it. Congratulations, she's beautiful.'

'Oh. . .' Katie blushed. 'Don't say that or my milk will start up. She *is* beautiful, isn't she?'

The occupational hazards involved in Ob practice nursing evidently increased in intensity and diversity in proportion to the duration of exposure, Nicole was forced to conclude as Katie, Alicia and a doting grandmother departed.

Examining the symptoms she was experiencing now—an inrush of tenderness, and intoxication with the sweet smell of baby scalp and a definite pleasure in being female—the only diagnosis she could come up with had a distinctly non-medical name.

I'm getting clucky, she thought. I wonder if there's an antidote. I wonder if I'd take it if there was. . .

CHAPTER SEVEN

'SHOULD we make it a weekend, then?'

The moment the words were out of Nicole's mouth she was appalled by them. So, evidently, was Richard.

'You mean, go away,' he clarified in an abrupt tone. 'For the whole weekend. Together. Stay somewhere. An inn, or something.' He stopped.

'Yes, something like that,' she agreed wretchedly. 'But, forget it. It was. . .I mean, just a spur-of-the-moment idea.'

'Was it?'

'Yes. I said it before I thought it, almost, and if you hate the idea. . .'

'No need to be hasty,' he drawled. 'I'd never want it said that I was a man who closed off his options, before fully examining them. Let's consider the pros and cons.'

'Oh, let's *not*, Richard,' she wailed.

'Well, I think we ought to,' he countered, maddeningly deliberate. 'I mean, you don't think there's a danger that this whole thing between us could get out of hand?'

'How could it possibly do that?' she bit at him, 'when you insist on. . .practically drafting a constitutional amendment every time something happens between us that doesn't quite fit your notions as to what's appropriate in a casual affair.'

'Are you saying a casual affair is no longer what you want?' There was both steel and silk in his voice, but she had the deeply rooted suspicion that neither of these qualities expressed what he was really feeling.

'A casual affair is quite definitely what I want,' she told him crisply.

Alone in her bed at Barb's house last night, she had dreamed of Colin again, and had woken in a clammy sweat. These dreams had been coming fairly often lately, and she wondered if it was her subconscious telling her to cool off with Richard—telling her that she was feeling trapped. When she was with Richard, though, that didn't seem to fit. She never felt trapped with him. This did *not* mean, however, that she never felt angry!

'What I *don't* want,' she finished now, 'is this endless nit-picking about it. I want to. . .just go with the flow.'

'And the flow is flowing towards a weekend away together?'

'Yes. No. . . Look! I just thought, as you'd said it was a bit of a drive to Hocking Hills and there was lots to see, that rather than just making it a day picnic. . . Forget it!'

He sat back, studying her. They were at the café at Mill Run Athletic Club on a Tuesday evening, having met up by chance in the pool during her long swim. Again, he had been maddening in his careful conclusion that adjourning here for a quick meal after their separate showers wouldn't be a heinous violation of these ridiculous *rules* that he seemed to be somehow so much more well-versed in than she was.

He was thirty-six. Maybe he'd had the same rules for the past fifteen years, with the red-headed Linda and a host of other gorgeous women, and that was why he was so clear on them. That was repellent, really, wasn't it? To be so cold-blooded? An affair should be a *hot*-blooded thing!

She glared at him and occupied her irritably restless fingers by twisting her hair up into a businesslike knot at the back of her head, lest he should think that its fluid undulation around her shoulders was any sort of an attempt to look seductive and coax him into this weekend-at-an-inn idea.

'Just *forget* it, Richard!' she repeated, knowing she was now flushing in her anger.

But, to her surprise—not necessarily her *pleasure*—he said decisively, 'No, let's do it. It's a great idea, actually. We can head off straight after work on Friday, and then I don't take over the on-call from Beth until nine on Sunday night. There's a list of Hocking Hills inns in the travel section of Sunday's *Dispatch*. I'll make some calls as soon as I get home. We'll have to hope there's been a cancellation, I expect, as it's the July Fourth weekend.'

'We could make it another time. . .'

'No, if we're going to do it, let's do it. I've been promising to take you to Hocking Hills.'

He picked his car keys off the table, tossed them in the air and caught them as if to punctuate his decision, then picked up his athletic bag and was off, leaving her open-mouthed in her seat.

'But, Richard. . .'

He was almost out of sight in the direction of the racquetball courts before she could get the words out.

Stopping, he turned slowly, and she saw that he was grinning. 'Your idea, Nic,' he reminded her, softly teasing. 'I'll call you tonight and let you know if we've got a reservation.'

And this time he really was gone. He hadn't kissed her, she calculated, in three days.

Friday began busy and didn't get better. Richard had squeezed in a seven-thirty a.m. surgical procedure at short notice, as he sometimes did on Fridays, and the patient wasn't fully prepped in time so it ran a little late, which meant they were scrambling all morning to keep on schedule with office appointments. In the back of her mind, too, Nicole was well aware that at least three huge, hot, pregnant ladies were ready—and desperately keen—to pop at any moment.

'Not before five o'clock, *please*!' she muttered to herself just before lunch.

Richard had managed to get them a booking at the Fallsview Inn in Hocking Hills, an hour or two's drive south-east of Columbus, and now that they'd both had a couple of days to get used to the idea they'd stopped expressing any overt scepticism about each other's motives and were very much looking forward to the weekend.

Nicole was, anyway.

It would be great to really get away for a couple of days as the heat and humidity were beginning to get her down in Barb's un-airconditioned house. And she had to assume that Richard was feeling the same because he certainly seemed to be in a good mood.

She was hoping to get away by half past four. Beth Kramer was taking the on-call from five o'clock onwards, and Richard would collect Nicole from her place shortly after that—provided he wasn't summoned to Labor and Delivery at a critical moment.

Their last patient had been scheduled only this morning for an examination to ascertain the exact status of her pregnancy after a suspected miscarriage, and it turned out to be one of those times when something that started out as fairly routine suddenly wasn't.

The first Nicole knew of it was Richard's voice, suddenly urgent as he called to her from room one, and she came dashing in from room two where she'd been tidying and replenishing supplies used during the day.

Richard was desperately trying to deal with a gush of blood, and when Nicole looked at the patient's face she guessed that shock was causing a swooping plunge in her blood pressure.

'It was a cervical pregnancy,' he told her quickly and quietly as they worked to get the bleeding under control. 'Quite rare. A mass of cells actually implanted in the cervix itself. It wasn't viable, of course, but the exam she had in the emergency room didn't pick this up.'

'It should have, surely?'

'New interns started this week,' he pointed out. 'Things are always a bit more difficult in July.'

'In Australia that happens in January.'

'Anyway, she began bleeding as soon as I tried to get a closer look at what it was.'

'This isn't right, is it?' Trina Palfrey asked faintly, trying to lift her head.

'No, it's not,' Richard answered frankly, 'but I've got the bleeding under control now, and Nicole will stay with you until you're feeling better. We'll make you some tea and find you something to eat. What did they tell you down in the ER?'

'Just that I must have miscarried because there was nothing on the ultrasound, no pregnancy ring or whatever. Only I hadn't had much bleeding and my sister thought that didn't seem quite right. She's a patient of Dr Kramer's so she said I should try and see someone here, and I managed to get you on a cancellation.'

'Which was good because you wouldn't have wanted to have this happen at home. Have you got someone with you?'

'Yes, my sister's waiting to take me home, thank goodness, because I don't feel as if I could drive.'

Mrs Palfrey had some more questions, worded very shakily as she sat up and sipped her tea, then it was just a matter of waiting until she felt strong enough to leave. With her more experienced sister for support, she seemed to be dealing with the pregnancy loss quite well.

'We'll try again,' she said. 'Maybe wait six months. I kind of accept now that there was never really a baby there. . .'

Ten to five.

'Are you packed?' Richard wanted to know, coming up to Nicole as she was loading the autoclave.

'Not quite.'

'Never mind. A bit of a late start. I've got a couple more things to do, but we should both be out of here by five-fifteen.'

'And I'm virtually done now.'

'As long as there's no call from—' The words weren't even out of his mouth when his pager sounded.

'Ha, ha,' Nicole drawled, as he strode to the phone. She watched him make the call, thinking to herself, Bridget Cleary? Torie Harris? Or Lashawn Brown?

It was none of the above. That was clear almost at once, and she couldn't help the little shiver that passed down her spine at the sight of his face. It was as if he'd suddenly gone on full alert, any awareness that he had wanted to get away promptly forgotten now.

His rapid monosyllables and medical shorthand didn't give away much, and the call was quite short, ending with a brisk, 'OK, I'll be right over.'

He seemed to remember Nicole only as he saw her standing there.

'Not a routine delivery?' she said.

'Anything but.' He hesitated. 'I have to go.'

'I know.'

'Look. . . Want to come? You may end up being involved anyway. . .if the mother survives.'

The chill in her spine came again, more strongly. 'Survives?'

'Major road trauma,' he explained tersely as they left the office suite and took the elevator. 'They've had her in surgery for several hours, apparently, fighting to stabilise her. The thing is, the pregnancy is only at about five and a half months.'

'Just "about"? That's not a very scientific measurement.'

'That's the first thing they want me to do—try and establish a more exact gestational age so they'll know if delivering now will give the baby any chance.'

He said nothing more until they reached the seventh

floor intensive care unit, outside which they both donned gowns and caps. Entering, it was immediately clear to both of them which was the patient they had come to see. There was a knot of medical people gathered in the entrance to the cubicle, and the group loosened a little to admit Richard and Nicole.

Glancing at name badges, there was only one she recognised—that of Dr William Hartman, one of Riverbank's top neonatologists. She had never met him but had spoken to him on the phone as he had taken on two premature babies delivered by Richard in recent months. The other three doctors would be trauma surgeons— brilliant people with incredibly demanding and very specialised roles. Two of them were arguing now.

'The bleeding in the brain—.'

'Has been dealt with.'

'But it looked massive.'

'That's immaterial,' the third surgeon came in. 'What concerns me now is the—'

'We've been over this, haven't we?' the first man said.

Then Dr Hartman came in, his voice like the low, ominous rumble of thunder in the distance. 'Look, do any of you guys think this patient can survive?'

There was silence, then a concert of reluctant negatives.

'Then, surely,' Dr Hartman went on, 'the only issue here is the viability of the baby. If Dr Gilbert and I can establish that there's at least some chance can this woman be maintained on life support for any length of time in order to improve that chance?'

Again there was silence, then the oldest of the doctors, Bradley Teague—a grey-haired man with rather thin lips and very tired eyes—spoke for all three of them. 'I doubt it,' he said. 'With aggressive treatment, we can probably buy you a few days, but after that. . .no. This body is just too badly injured to be able to nourish a baby.'

'The baby is still alive now, I presume,' Richard came in.

'We heard a heartbeat,' Dr Jeffrey Grey confirmed, 'and saw some movements while we were in the abdominal cavity. No obvious evidence of foetal injury but. . .' He shrugged helplessly.

To Nicole this was all horribly cold-blooded, but perhaps it had to be. The first sight these men had of a trauma patient was often almost inhuman, resembling a lion's fresh kill more than a living being, if the injuries were very serious. Perhaps they couldn't be blamed for talking so coolly and technically.

'Can we get an ultrasound scanner up here?' Richard wanted to know.

'On its way,' Dr Teague answered laconically.

'And why us?' Richard asked. 'That's something I didn't have time to get clear on the phone. Why Will and myself?'

'Next of kin's request,' Dr Teague supplied. 'It's a sister in Boston. I gather she's on her way. She asked that a top neonatologist and obstetrician be brought in. We thought of you.'

Richard and Dr Hartman exchanged small, wry smiles. 'Flattered,' Richard murmured.

'She's a doctor herself, apparently.'

Instinctively, they all turned to the bed, where aggressive life-support technology totally swamped the damaged figure which lay there, closely watched over by a strongly built nurse. Nicole knew that everyone must be thinking just as she was—that this woman didn't look like someone who would have a doctor for a sister.

She had the pallor and thinness of someone who hadn't looked after herself properly for years, and there were several places on her undersized limbs where crude, amateur tattoos showed their blue-black stains. Nicole identified a misshapen rose, two different men's

names and an obscenity adorned and somewhat dis-
guised with vine leaves.

The fingers of the motionless left hand, from which
an IV line and a pulse oximeter snaked, were adorned
with black nail polish, though the nails themselves were
badly bitten. Cheap hair bleach had grown out about
two inches to reveal dark roots, as if she'd stopped
bleaching it when she realised she was pregnant.

Which was interesting when you thought about it.

On an impulse, Nicole asked, 'Was there any evidence
of drug or alcohol abuse in her system?'

Oops. Since she didn't really have a professional role
in this august group she probably shouldn't have spoken,
but Richard deflected attention from her quickly, by
saying with a frown, 'Yes, I was about to get to that
myself. Did she, Brad?'

'Interestingly, no,' the senior surgeon answered.
'Defying the obvious stereotype a bit there. I'd say
there's definitely been a good bit of it in her past, though.
And you should have seen how she was dressed when
she was brought in.'

'Let's keep our priorities straight,' Will Hartman
came in. 'If there's no evidence of substance abuse then
that gives the baby a better chance, and that's all we
really need to know at the moment.'

'The scanner's here,' said the ICU's head nurse,
coming over to the group.

Then she stepped aside as a technician and an orderly
wheeled in the big machine and began to set it up, almost
blocking the cubicle off completely. There was a tense
few minutes as it was readied for operation, with Dr
Teague conferring with the patient's nurse in the background.

'Blood pressure and heart rate both dropping. . .'
Nicole heard.

'We may have to go in and try another repair to the
lung. . .'

The scanner was ready now, but first Richard took a tape measure and stretched it vertically along the unmistakable swell of the dying patient's pregnancy. 'The height of the fundus is consistent with that five-and-a-half-month estimate, give or take. A bit smaller? Twenty-three weeks? But, then, she's small to begin with. Where did we get that figure from, anyway?'

'The sister,' Dr Grey supplied, 'but she says it may not be very accurate. It's based purely on what the patient told her when they last saw each other about two months ago. "Three and a half months gone" the sister was told then.'

'Do these people have names?' Will Hartman suddenly said impatiently. 'I keep hearing "the sister, the patient".'

'Er, Chattie?' Dr Teague turned vaguely to the nurse, who was studying her monitors.

'This is Heather,' Chattie Macarthur said. 'Heather Powell. And the sister is Jennifer.'

'Lovely!' Dr Teague growled. 'Heather and Jennifer, like a debutantes' ball. Now we can all be friends.'

But if Will Hartman felt derided it didn't show. Privately, Nicole approved of his attitude. Names were important.

Richard had stayed out of the whole thing, concentrating on the matter at hand. He had been spreading clear gel on Heather Powell's exposed abdomen, just below a series of huge dressings and drainage tubes, and now he was asking, 'Can we have some fluid put in through that catheter? We'll get a much better picture with a full bladder.'

The head nurse, June Ames, had anticipated the request and was ready with a bag of saline. When it was put in Richard began to pass the probe across the abdomen, while Dr Hartman looked on intently and the other doctors craned to see as well. Nicole, standing well in the background, saw only the grey, grainy sweep of the picture, which revealed the shadowy outline of a head and the notched vertebrae of the spine.

It took some minutes to make a thorough examination, using the computerised equipment to make measurements of several parts of the tiny baby's body as well as studying the degree of development of organs and limbs.

Finally Richard turned to the group. 'I'd say about twenty-four weeks, wouldn't you, Will?'

'Plus a couple of days if we're lucky,' the neonatologist agreed.

'Minus a couple of days if we're not.'

'Certainly no older than about twenty-five weeks, and that's optimistic. I think it's a girl, by the way, but I wouldn't stake money on it.'

'Then there's a chance,' Bradley Teague summarised. 'But if we could buy you a few more days—'

'It could make the difference between a baby that ultimately attains normal development and a baby with lifelong chronic problems,' Dr Hartman said.

'Or a baby that dies.'

'Yes.'

'And there's no evidence of foetal injury?'

'Amazingly, none that's apparent,' Richard said. 'The heart rate is good, and there was movement, as you probably all saw.'

'Then we'll buy you the time, if we possibly can.'

'I'm not on call this weekend,' Richard said. 'Beth Kramer is covering for the whole practice. You know her, Will.'

'She's very good.' He nodded.

'She is, and I'll let her know what's going on in case she does have to deliver before Sunday night when I'll be back.'

'Let's hope we can keep her for you,' Dr Teague said.

'The sister's here.' June Ames had returned to drain the fluid that had been pumped into Heather Powell's abdomen. 'I mean Jennifer...' She glanced uneasily at

Will Hartman. 'Dr Powell, I guess. I've got her waiting outside. Who wants to talk to her?'

'I will,' Dr Hartman volunteered, surprising everyone.

While recognised as a brilliant neonatologist, Nicole knew, he was widely rumoured not to know the meaning of the words 'personal life'. Though, apparently, he dealt with bereaved or frightened parents and relatives sensitively when it was clearly his duty it wasn't a job he normally jumped at. Well, no one did. It was one of the hardest things a doctor ever had to do.

Eyebrows were raised all round as he quietly left the unit, and Brad Teague drawled sarcastically, 'I guess he really likes the name Jennifer.'

Nicole saw Chattie Macarthur roll her eyes, and the two of them exchanged a sad sort of smile and looked down at the patient.

She wouldn't see this woman again, Nicole realised. Heather. . . She'd hear about her death, and about her baby. She wondered what her sister was like. . .

Richard's role was finished now. He held up his gloved hands and said quietly to Nicole, 'Going to get rid of these and wash. Meet you just outside?'

So she waited for him there and saw Dr Hartman over by the windows that looked north-east across the highway to the river through the humid haze of the late afternoon. He was talking to Jennifer Powell.

They made a heartrending picture when you knew, as Nicole did, what he must be saying to her. He was a tall man, and Dr Powell was rather petite, so that he was bending his head down to her, not touching her but perhaps wanting to as there was something about the stiff set of her shoulders that betrayed the emotion she was struggling to contain and almost seemed to demand the solace of someone's gently placed hand.

Richard came out and they went together to the elevator so that she couldn't see Dr Hartman and Heather Powell's sister any more.

'You didn't really need to be there,' Richard said, raking her in rough assessment with his dark eyes. 'Sorry. I should have just sent you home.'

'No,' she answered. 'I'm glad I was. This way, when she's close to death and you get called to deliver her baby, I'll know what's going on and I can. . .I don't know. . .send a prayer along with you?'

'Let's leave it for now, put it aside,' he suggested quietly. 'It doesn't help anyone if we brood on these things. I'll be at your place as soon as I'm ready, OK?'

They went out into the hot heavy air and separated to go to their respective parking lots. He picked her up from home half an hour later, dressed in cuffed khaki shorts and a black knit shirt, while she wore matching shorts and blouse in embroidered blue chambray.

He called Beth Kramer on his car phone as soon as they reached the highway to let her know that she might be called in to handle the emergency delivery over the weekend. Then he called the Fallsview Inn to say that they'd be a little late for the evening meal they had ordered.

'We're on our way,' he promised, 'but there was a medical emergency. I'm a doctor, you see. . .'

It took both of them most of the drive to really leave the hospital behind.

It was only a little cooler in the hills. Only a little less humid, too.

'I'm grateful for the air-conditioning,' Richard pronounced on Saturday morning as they emerged from the room to find the day's heat already apparent in the air outside.

They'd had a pleasant night. Slow, unambitious, with both of them concerned only with sloughing off the fatigue and tension of the working week. It had been eight o'clock by the time they'd sat down to dinner, and the chilled cucumber soup, leafy salad and Cajun-style fish, followed by hazelnut ice cream for dessert, had been both refreshing and nourishing.

Early to bed. Not quite as early to sleep. . .

And early to rise, despite earnest intentions to sleep in. They were both too used to their six-thirty alarms. Nicole chose the inn's lighter continental breakfast, but Richard betrayed a careless confidence in his immunity to cholesterol and elected to consume the full American breakfast buffet of scrambled eggs, bacon, sausages, home fries, biscuits and gravy—and even a generous raft of waffles, soaking in syrup and butter.

'Don't often do this,' he said, 'but, what the heck, this is a vacation.'

'I'm glad,' Nicole replied a little faintly.

'That it's a vacation?'

'That you don't do it very often. The breakfast, that is. I'm finding it a bit of a challenge to watch, at this hour, actually. Particularly the. . .um. . .gravy.'

A gulp of orange juice immediately dispelled her wave of vague nausea and she quickly forgot it as he pulled out a map, after agreeing. 'Yes, the gravy is nicer in anticipation than reality, I must confess. I think I'm cured of it for the next five years at least. Now, today's hiking options. . .'

They argued very amicably over the possibilities for a while and ended up with an ambitious itinerary. Too ambitious, perhaps. She was exhausted by the time they returned at four to their starting point at Cedar Falls, and was very content to sit in the shade and feel the wafts of spray drifting across from the plunging water, made quite forceful after a heavy thunderstorm—typical for Ohio at this time of year—which had passed through in the early hours of the morning.

It was quite hot. Even in the less humid hills, the air was far heavier than she was used to. She could almost see the haze of steamy moisture in it, hovering like a pale mist amongst the thickly leafed trees.

'I thought that thunderstorm last night would clear it,' she said to Richard, 'but it hasn't.'

'Not in central Ohio, generally,' he laughed. 'That's another weather saying we have. If it's humid wait till it rains. . .then it'll be worse.'

'I've noticed all your central Ohio weather sayings tend to involve things getting worse,' she said with an accusing frown. 'I'm whacked!'

'Ice cream, maybe? We could drive back to Old Man's Cave, where there's a kiosk.'

'Just water sounds better. Plain, ice-cold water!'

He looked at her narrowly. 'You all right, Nic?'

'Fine. Overdid my back a bit.'

'Hurting?'

'Hmm.'

'Take something. . .'

'Well. . .'

'Pain is tiring,' he insisted with authority. 'People don't think of that, but struggling against pain is exhausting. I've got painkillers in the car.'

'OK, then,' she conceded.

He stood up at once to go and fetch them, as well as some water, and she felt rather deliciously cosseted— until she realised that this was how she was feeling, whereupon she immediately rebelled against it and jumped up to go and meet him at the water fountain.

It wasn't nearly as far as the car so she arrived first and was just beaten to a drink by a very pregnant and hot-looking woman, who was saying to her four-year-old, 'Come on, Heather, I'll lift you up.'

Heather. The name of that poor young woman who lay in Riverbank Hospital, kept alive by machine but still losing that last elemental fight against death. And this pregnant woman was like those she saw dozens of every week.

'No escape,' Nicole muttered darkly, and the woman turned and frowned.

'From the heat,' she appended with a quick smile.

'You should walk a mile in *my* shoes!' the woman said crossly, then turned to her daughter. 'Don't *kick* me, for goodness' sake, Heather!'

Richard's painkillers helped, and so did dinner, but it was rather rich and enormous so perhaps it wasn't surprising that she seemed to dream all night.

And what dreams!

Blame it, too, on their love-making, which seemed to have some particular magic to it tonight, perhaps because they'd spent an uninterrupted day and a half together now, away from home, and had been put very much in tune by their day outdoors.

Returning to their room at nine after half an hour of lazy talking in the rocking chairs grouped on a very private porch, they showered together—another first in their relationship, actually—and the way he turned it into a seduction was quite deliberate, lathering the soap all over her and washing away the day's grime in sensuous circles with his hands from places which probably hadn't got very dirty at all. . .

She returned the favour, loving the contrast of soap and skin and male hair—loving the slip of their wet bodies together as he took her in his arms—loving the way his kiss tasted of the cool running water that streamed down their faces.

'Have you noticed that the towels here are *huge*,' he murmured in her ear after he turned off the water, wrapped one around her and dried her—tenderly at first, as if she'd been a crystal wine glass, then with a playful roughness that had her attacking him with another towel seconds later. Finally, both of them chased each other onto the big, wooden sleigh-bed. . .

Back to the subject of the dreams. They began after about an hour of the light, lazy sleep that follows passion, and tonight they were inexorable, endless, vivid, flamboyant, obsessive.

But when she woke in the morning to Richard's sensual touch they instantly dissolved, like a heat mirage in the middle of a grey metal road, so that she was left with the uneasy knowledge that she'd had them. . .or they'd had her. . .but now she couldn't remember what they'd been about.

And the insistent, familiar evidence of Richard's arousal set her own body so quickly on fire that the dream images were chased even further to the back of her mind.

They planned an easier day today. Just an exploration of Cantwell Cliffs after a late departure from Fallsview and a restful picnic, supplied by the inn's kitchen. The heat and humidity seemed stronger, and it was good to reach the shade of the overhanging cliffs.

Breakfasting late, Nicole had been tempted by the eggs and bacon, but that now seemed like a mistake. They were sitting heavily in her stomach as she walked.

Then, when they reached the cool bowl of the cave-like overhang at the bottom of the cliff path, she saw the same pregnant woman who had been at Cedar Falls yesterday, and suddenly she remembered what all those dreams last night had been about—herself, huge and heavy, sleepy and hot, vague and dithery and restless, yet somehow at the same time ripe and thoroughly cosseted and utterly happy.

And all at once it came together in her mind with the flash of a chemical reaction—the meaning of the dreams, her fatigue and those moments of nausea quite evident to her now.

I'm pregnant. . .

CHAPTER EIGHT

'EVERYTHING all right, Nic?'

'Oh, yes. Fine. It's just hot,' Nicole lied brightly.

'Is a bit,' Richard agreed easily. 'Could be building to a storm. . .'

He said nothing further, apparently satisfied with her answer, and stretched his long legs to clamber onto a rock and examine a lurid fungus, which left her free to pursue the desperate, feverish skittering of her thoughts.

Pregnant.

No! Surely it had to be impossible. She'd been using contraception faithfully. But it wasn't a hundred per cent reliable, and they'd certainly been giving themselves enough chances to buck the odds. Still, wasn't she panicking too soon? She was only a couple of days late. But those dreams—as if her body was trying to tell her something which *it* knew but *she* didn't. And her fatigue, those moments of nausea, the tenderness in her breasts.

I am. I can't kid myself. I am.

And Richard would be appalled.

She couldn't think clearly about it at all. What would it mean? When was the baby due? Would he want her to consider a termination? She *couldn't*! Due. . .? She calculated, using a simple, familiar formula. First day of last menstrual period plus seven days plus nine months. Mid-March. Which was when she was due to end this exchange with Barb Zelinsky and go home.

That wouldn't work. Richard wouldn't want her to stay that long, swelling visibly, having everyone wonder or—worse, perhaps—*guess* who had got her that way. She'd have to leave as soon as possible. It was the only way.

Richard would be appalled, angry. . .

He'd made it so clear that he didn't even want the normal entanglement in each other's lives that came with any halfway serious relationship, let alone this closest and most intricate, unbreakable bond of all. Would he think she'd been lying to him all along about her own need for space, telling him what he wanted to hear while secretly planning this classic form of entrapment? What a horrible, laughable irony *that* would be!

Look at him now—that fit, relaxed, totally capable and very virile body moving over the rocks. He had turned now to see where she was. He had no idea. . .

He would be appalled!

It never occurred to her to try and get away with not telling him. She just wasn't made that way—couldn't disguise her turmoil for five minutes, let alone for the weeks it would take her to plan and carry out her departure from Riverbank Ob/Gyn and from Columbus itself.

She was already starting to think about it, trying to plan the right setting and mood and lead-up in a vain attempt to make it seem less of a disaster, when he suddenly seemed to forget about fungi and fauna and came up to her with a frown to say tenderly, 'What is it, Nic? What's wrong?'

His hands were pressed softly around the knobs of her shoulders, and his face was tilted down to her, brushing her forehead with a kiss and then seeking her lips gently. She tried to respond to his kiss but couldn't. She was just too shaky and distracted and emotional.

'You're miles away, aren't you?' he whispered. 'Not here with me in spirit at all. And you look miserable. Tell me! I'm sure I can help.'

And she was too overwhelmed to even consider softening the blow.

'I'm sorry, Richard,' she said through dry lips, looking up at him, then instantly down again because she couldn't bear to meet that dark gaze. 'This is appalling.

You're going to wish you'd never laid eyes on me. I've just realised this morning. . .I think I must be pregnant.'

For quite a long time, with his hands stiffened on her shoulders, he didn't say anything at all. Then, woodenly, he said, 'What makes you think so?' He released her, stepping back a pace.

She outlined the evidence carefully, trying to keep it rational, as she would have if this had been a patient they were discussing together, and he nodded. 'You could be, I suppose.'

'I definitely could be! I—I am, I'm sure of it!'

'And you've suspected since. . .?'

'Just now. Half an hour ago. I'm sorry.' Again, she dared to look at that glittering gaze for only a moment, before staring down again at her damp, twisting fingers. 'I—I didn't do it on purpose. This is as ghastly for me as it is for you.'

'Is it?' His voice was still oddly expressionless.

'Yes! Oh, you *can't* think I did it on purpose!' she beseeched, desperately trying to reach him. 'It's the last thing I want, given the nature of our relationship.'

She felt a bead of sweat gather just below her collarbone and travel down to find the hot valley between her breasts. The air was so horribly heavy today. It was as if she could scarcely breathe, and the lump which had formed in her throat now didn't help.

'Things like this tend to change the nature of a relationship,' he pointed out drily.

'*No*!' she insisted wildly. 'I knew that's what you'd think. I'm not asking for *anything* from you, Richard. I'll have to leave, of course, go back to Australia and have the baby there.'

'You don't want me to arrange an abortion?' Was that his *professional* tone, for heaven's sake? 'You know our practice doesn't do them, but we do get asked for referrals and—'

'No!' She shuddered. 'I'm sorry! That's going too

far! My God, Richard, to suggest it in that cold-blooded way. . .'

'I wasn't trying to be cold-blooded. I was trying to help. To find out what you want.' He was still talking in that dead, wooden tone. The strong planes of his face barely moved as he spoke. 'I'm very. . .interested in what you want, Nic.'

'Well, I want to have the baby and. . .and I want to keep it, too—'

'You've really thought this all out, haven't you?' he accused, running a hand back through his hair to sweep the damp tendrils away from his high forehead.

But she answered miserably, 'Not really, no. I'm— I'm just going by what feels right. Are you saying—?' She stopped, and dared to really look at him for the first time, having been too fraught—and definitely too frightened—to do so before.

Now she was horrified at what she saw. He paced restlessly for a moment with his back to her, then wheeled around, stopping at a point where the heat hazy sunlight fell on him, although he was surrounded by shade. He was quite white, the firm, sensuous fullness of his lips stretched into two thin lines, and his black eyes burned. The effort he needed to maintain control was clearly huge, and she didn't dare to complete her sentence—had forgotten, anyway, what she'd been going to say.

'This is unbearable, isn't it?' he rasped finally.

'Yes.'

'Maybe we'd better do a pregnancy test before we torture each other any further on the issue,' he suggested, the bitterness in his voice very apparent now. 'You're only two days late, after all.'

'That makes sense,' she agreed shakily, knowing, just *knowing* that the test would be positive and wondering if it was a male fetish or an obstetric one to want to see the evidence with his own eyes.

'We should head back now, anyway.' He glanced at the hot, heavy pall of the sky revealed through the leafy trees overhead and the sweat glistened on his temples. 'There's definitely a storm coming. We'll eat in the car, go straight up to the office, do the test and go from there.'

'OK, but not the office,' she answered quickly. 'You've always said—and I've agreed—to keep it separate. Dr Kramer's on this weekend, too, and you know she often goes up there between close deliveries rather than drive home.'

'Sure,' he said. 'We'll pick up a test at the supermarket, then.'

They ate in the car as they drove, and the tasty and imaginative picnic items might have been stale, greasy French fries for all the pleasure they took in the food.

That storm was building, lying leaden grey on the horizon to the west and looming closer and closer. They didn't talk, and the tension and distance between them were almost as palpable as the heavy air. Nicole had never realised until now, when it was suddenly absent, just how relaxed and strong had been the connection between them.

If asked, she'd have said it was all bed—sex— because that was so often at the heart of the time they spent together, but now she realised just how much more there was and what a dark hole was left when it was gone—the honesty, which had been almost dangerous at the beginning, the humour, the pleasurable arguing over plans.

Daring to glance at him, but only briefly, as he drove, she thought, He's so incredibly distant. I have no idea what he's thinking or feeling beyond the fact that he's as angry as that storm. I can't *bear* this! What a fool I was to think that something like this. . .something that started out so casually. . .would be better than the claustrophobia I felt with Colin. It's worse!

Thunder was rumbling close at hand by the time he pulled into the parking lot in front of the supermarket at the corner of North Broadway, and she had to forestall him as he started to open the driver's side door.

'I'll get it.'

'Don't be ridiculous, Nic.'

But she picked up her bag and didn't listen to his protest. 'I'll get it, Richard, OK?' One thing he *couldn't* accuse her of was trying to draw him into an involvement with this, and she would prove it to him from the very beginning by paying for the pregnancy test herself.

She was shaking by the time she returned to the car, clutching the grey plastic bag containing her purchase. His gaze swept over the bag as if to say, Ashamed? Had to hide it? And, of course, she was.

Ashamed of what, though?

They reached her place two minutes later, still silent as they climbed from his car.

'I'll wait here on the porch,' he told her. She nodded, slung her overnight bag onto the living-room floor and went up to the bathroom alone. She heard the porch swing start to creak to and fro as she climbed the stairs, feeling a sudden bizarre kinship to a condemned prisoner on the way to the gallows.

It didn't take long to set up the test, then she did as she always did at the office and left the room while the necessary interval of time elapsed, not wanting to hang there in suspense while the colour on the testing strip slowly changed.

The wait was only a minute long. She counted it through in a tight murmur to keep panic at bay—'Thousand and one, thousand and two, thousand and three'— as she'd learned to measure out seconds as a child, then went back into the bathroom on cotton-wool legs.

Negative.

Negative! The testing strip was still uncompromisingly, unmistakably white.

Shaking even more as the strength returned to her legs and her heartbeat slowed, her mind had room for only one thought—this would take that awful, hunted, desperate, angry look from Richard's face. He would be incredibly, unutterably relieved! Things would be back the way they should be again—so warm and passionate and *right*. . .

She ran down to him, scarcely aware that the clouds had opened overhead and wild, wind-blown rain was cascading down. He had been sitting on the porch swing, pushing himself idly back and forth with one foot— creak-creak, creak-creak—but now he stopped and stood, saw the new life in her and the smile on her face and came eagerly forward to sweep her into his arms.

'Nic! Oh, Nic! You look. . . Does this mean you've found out you—?'

'Yes!' she nodded, sighing gustily, then almost laughed. 'Yes! It was negative! I could cry with relief, and to think of what I've put you through today for nothing! We could have stayed at Hocking Hills and enjoyed our picnic before the storm. I'm so sorry, Richard!'

But he had stiffened and now he pulled away, to stare at her with his black eyes like icy slits. 'My God,' he said. 'I'm just throwing precious stones into a bottomless well with you, aren't I, Nic? I thought I was starting to understand you, and better than you understood yourself, too, but, hell, was I ever wrong! If even *this* little episode couldn't do it. . . Congratulations! You are one scary lady! You know what you want and nothing's going to bring you to feel any differently. It makes me shiver, frankly!'

She thought that was just words, and then she saw that he *was* shivering, the skin standing out in bumps all over his arms and bringing those fine dark hairs up to attention. Or was it the storm? The wind was blowing the rain onto the porch now, cooling the air for the moment and spraying them both with droplets.

She felt quite numb and sick, as if she'd just got off a roller-coaster. Somehow she had read him very wrongly and even now she didn't quite understand how. He wasn't waiting to help her find out, though. He'd already dived off the porch and down the steps, ducking his head against the storm but drenched within seconds nevertheless.

'Richard, wait!'

He turned. 'What for?'

'So we can talk. I—'

'There's nothing to say. I've been wasting your time, Nic, and you've been wasting mine. Probably I'm to blame. I was arrogant enough to think that I knew what you needed better than you did.'

'And you thought I needed a *baby*? I—I don't understand,' she called pitifully, but with the roar of the rain he didn't even seem to hear, and at that moment the tornado warning siren keened into life with its eerie wailing.

Ignoring it completely, he had driven off seconds later, but Nicole couldn't abandon the scene that easily. She stood on the porch until the storm passed, positively daring a tornado to come and blast her away, and when she went upstairs an hour later to change out of her damp clothing, she found that her period had started.

One day too late. If it had happened this time yesterday she never would have had that pregnancy scare, and why hadn't she remembered what Darla Hogan had said about it—'One of the occupational hazards of Ob nursing!' And if she hadn't had the pregnancy scare, she wouldn't have alienated Richard by—

I'm in love with him.

It was so blindingly obvious that it sent her to sprawl on the couch, moaning in pain. Why hadn't she known? Why hadn't she seen it weeks ago when it was so obvious in her every response to him?

That was easy enough to answer. Because the relationship had come so naturally to her under its false guise of 'no strings attached' that she'd never had to question what she felt. She had just enjoyed it, and love had grown out of it unnoticed because, after Colin, she still somehow thought that the emotion of love had to come with a sense of confinement, suffocation, possession.

If Richard had approached her in that way, had tried to bind their lives together with the trappings of dependence and domesticity, she would have run a mile and never let him get close, but because he'd been so vocal and so unwavering about not wanting commitment she'd felt safe and *this* had happened.

He'd laugh if he knew.

Did he know? she suddenly wondered. Had he seen it in her face, somehow, just then when she'd come out to him on the porch—before she had realised the truth herself? Or had he seen it this morning in the way she had reacted to the idea of pregnancy?

'I've been wasting your time, Nic, and you've been wasting mine,' he had said. But how did that fit with her negative pregnancy test? Was he arrogant enough to want to leave her with a permanent legacy of their relationship while he walked away from it free? Or was he just disgusted—in a professional sense, perhaps— that she seemed so lacking in maternal fervour?

'It was for you, Richard, you bastard, that I wanted not to be pregnant,' she whispered to the empty room. 'For me. . .'

For herself—she hugged her arms around her slender body, aching with loss and vividly reliving the sense of sleepy, expectant happiness that had coloured last night's dreams—for herself the thought that for half a day she'd believed herself to be carrying his baby, and hadn't realised what a joy that would be until the illusion was gone, was suddenly too miserably sad and ironic to bear.

*   *   *

'Hello?'

'Richard?'

'Yes,' he said wearily into the phone. It was a male
voice that had spoken, clipped and professional and
tired. Will Hartman, he suddenly realised, and sat up
straighter on his leather couch. 'Yes, Will?'

'She's deteriorating, and the baby's heart rate has
started to slow. I think you'd better come in.'

'I'll be there.'

'We'll get her prepped for a C-section. This weekend
has been bloody. . .'

It had been, Richard thought. Truly bloody, and he
hadn't even been near the hospital. Now the inevitable
end to the tragedy of Heather Powell almost loomed as
a relief since he knew it had to come one way or the
other. He *didn't* need to sit here any longer, thinking
pointless, circular thoughts about Nicole.

He changed quickly into scrubs and left the house, a
little bemused to find his normally quiet street unac-
countably lined with parked cars bumper to bumper until
he suddenly remembered that the July Fourth fireworks
were taking place in nearby Whetstone Park tonight.
The park would be crowded.

The afternoon storm had, for once, preceded a slight
cool change and the atmosphere was now clear and the
air less heavy than usual. The sky was almost dark—it
was just on ten—and as he slid into the driver's seat
the first burst of colour and noise came, with red, white
and blue stars cascading towards the dark canopy of
trees to the north-west of his house.

He didn't pause to appreciate the sight, and was outside the door of obstetric operating room one within
minutes. The place seemed full as he entered and the OR
lights even brighter than usual, reflecting off a couple of
faces which were grey with weariness. Will Hartman
was here. The whole team from Neonatal Intensive Care,
in fact, waited to whisk the baby down the corridor in

a transport isolette within minutes of the birth. . .provided the tiny human being survived that long.

But who was this petite, dark-haired young woman with the blue sheen of fatigue beneath her huge eyes? She looked vaguely familiar. . .

Will Hartman stepped forward and answered Richard's unspoken question in a quick murmured aside. 'Dr Powell. The patient's sister. She wants to be here, but I've told her it's your call. She hasn't left the hospital all weekend. . .'

'I have no problem with it,' he answered slowly, 'if you think she can handle it.'

'I think it's the *only* way she can handle it,' Will answered.

They both glanced towards her now. She had gone up close to the inert form lying on the table, a life that was sustained—and only by a thread—with technology which hadn't even existed when most of the people in this room were born, and she was saying something in a low voice. Saying goodbye? They couldn't hear the words, but there was something about the tone and her stance that suggested the making of a vow.

'She's been a problem all her life,' Will Hartman said. 'Heather Powell, that is. Dr Powell has been telling me about it. Drugs, prostitution, stealing from their parents. Apparently she started to clean up her act a bit when she got pregnant, but Jennifer didn't seem confident that it would have lasted. She seems to feel. . . almost a sort of peace about it, as if her sister has been saved now from a lot worse further down the line.'

'And yet this isn't the end of the line because there's going to be a baby,' Richard pointed out.

'Yes, well. . .' Will answered, and they both had the same thought. If the baby lives.

Richard didn't waste any more time. Under these circumstances, the surgery was purely a technical procedure. It was like the original Caesarean births, he realised—bringing a living child from a dying mother. It didn't take long, and his main role was to bring the baby out as quickly and carefully as possible in order to minimise the birth trauma. At the very threshhold of viability like this, any pressure on the skull could cause dangerous bleeding in the brain and a careless squeeze could leave a major bruise on these tiny limbs.

The moment the baby was born—and it was, indeed, a girl, as he'd thought from the ultrasound scan—the neonatal team took the focus. They checked the heart rate and bagged the lungs to get breathing started—at which point there was a surprisingly lusty cry—before passing a tube down to carry oxygen directly to the lungs.

Richard didn't try to involve himself with the child. He'd only have been in the way. Instead, he closed the incision carefully, knowing that even in death this woman had the right to be treated with dignity and expertise. He was aware, though, that the baby was being successfully and quickly resuscitated, its gestational age falling if not at their most optimistic estimate of twenty-five weeks then only a day or two short of that. At this point, the outlook for this tiny girl's survival and long-term health was actually better than they'd feared, but there was a long way to go.

The NICU team had left by the time he finished, and Dr Teague had arrived to make the formal decision to switch off life support before Heather Powell's deterioration made this action academic. Turning to discard his gloves, Richard saw that Jennifer Powell was still in the operating room, her exhaustion and strain even more apparent now but her bearing calm and controlled.

She came up to him as he made for the door. 'Thank you.'

'There wasn't much I could do beyond—'

'For treating her with respect,' Jennifer Powell finished, quietly firm about her need to say this. 'The way you repaired the incision. My sister and I were both adopted, from different mothers, and she had had a bad start in life that she was never able to overcome. I'll always remember that she was allowed to keep what dignity she could at the end, and I'm glad you were called in. Teresa Mary has had the best possible start to her life now, and I intend to make sure that it continues that way.'

'Keep me posted,' he said.

'I will.'

'I mean that,' he insisted, with a degree of emotion that he was usually careful not to feel in these situations. What was it? The fact that he was unusually raw after the ghastly day with Nicole, perhaps.

'I mean it, too,' Jennifer Powell answered. 'Teresa is going to need breast milk—'

'There are special feeding formulas for premature—'

'Breast milk,' the dark, petite woman repeated very firmly. 'Preferably from a mother who also delivered prematurely. If there's anyone in your practice who fits the bill and who'd be willing to donate. . .'

'I'll check.'

'Thanks. Not urgent. I expect she'll be on IV nutrition for a while.' There was a pale smile. Firm, though, and confident. Jennifer Powell wasn't even entertaining the possibility that her tiny niece might not make it. She turned back to her adoptive sister for a final private goodbye now that things were quiet.

Richard left and saw, to his amazement, as he came out into the night that the fireworks were still going on across the river. The end of one life and the start of another, all in the time it took to shoot a few spectacular chemicals into the air. This profession of his was a bit much at times, but when drama like this happened on top of a definitely disastrous weekend off. . .

It was tempting, at the moment, to take a leaf out of Will Hartman's book and wed himself to his work. That was very possibly as close to the questionable institution of marriage as he would ever get. A green and pink starburst spread like a parachute in the sky and he greeted it with a tired and very cynical smile.

Swimming had a certain anaesthetic value. This evening was Nicole's third session this week, and she was well into her second mile when normally she stopped at one. She was tiring rapidly, though, and thought to herself as she approached the end of Mill Run's outdoor pool with her smooth Australian crawl, Two more backstroke and I'll call it quits.

But when she was within two yards of the smooth, tiled end wall her strength suddenly gave out altogether, and she closed her eyes and let herself drift until she touched the end. No more.

She pushed onto her back and floated for a few minutes, looking up into the slightly hazy blue of the early evening sky. The fatigue was pleasant. It kept her from thinking. And the water was delightfully cool as it buoyed her up. Then she realised that another swimmer was approaching in her lane and she was blocking his path so she stretched forward to the aluminium ladder and pulled herself out of the water. . .to meet Richard.

His hair was damp from the shower but his compact black swimming shorts were dry so he had probably been working out in the gym until a short while ago. She remembered their little spat a few months ago over whether to provide each other with schedules of their planned sessions here, and wished for the first time that they'd taken the ridiculous notion seriously.

It wasn't the first time they'd met here by chance in recent weeks, but those meetings hadn't mattered. They'd greeted each other and smiled in what she only now recognised had been a deliciously conspiratorial way, a way that silently shared the secret of their affair. Now. . .

'Hello, Nicole.'

'I've just finished.' She felt intensely aware of her own body, the navy and white suit he had bought for her still streaming with water and clinging to her so closely that it was like a second skin.

'So I see,' he answered, flicking a rapid glance over her so that she was painfully conscious of how the air on her wet skin had tightened her breasts into hard little buds. He knew her body so well, and for the first time this made her vulnerable. . .

He explained casually, 'I've had a session in the gym.'

He flung a towel onto one of the lounging chairs arranged in a row behind him and stepped past her to crouch and spring fluidly into the water, not bothering with the steps. He waited for a swimmer to pass then set off himself, his stroke clean, efficient and powerful and his kick straight-legged so that he looked as smooth as a seal in the water.

He had already overtaken two other swimmers by the time he reached the far end of the pool, but now he stopped and stood for a moment with his back to her. She could see the muscles in his back rippling as he lifted his hands to sweep streaming hair back off his face, but that wasn't really why he had stopped. He was catching his breath because he hadn't intended just to enter the pool and sprint off like that.

He'd been escaping her.

It was Wednesday night, which meant they'd spent three working days together since Sunday's stormy parting, and he'd avoided her as much as possible in the context of work, too. There she could say nothing about it—couldn't afford to give away in the slightest what she was feeling in case someone else noticed—but here it was different, and she suddenly knew that they had to talk about this.

He had turned now and was coming back down the pool, using a powerful butterfly stroke. Probably he thought that he'd given her enough time to dry off a little and go, and his narrow-eyed surprise when he saw her, standing there at the end of the pool and leaning down to him, with her hands pressed flat between her lower thighs confirmed this.

'Richard?' It came out unsteadily.

Still dripping, she was starting to feel cold as the breeze blew through her wet suit.

'What is it?'

'We need to talk.'

'Do we?' he challenged.

'OK,' she amended. '*I* need to talk. To you.'

'Now, I expect.'

'Well, should we do it at the office?' she suggested sweetly. 'Perhaps you'll have a cancellation and you can squeeze me in.'

'OK, I get the point.' He pressed his hands on the rim of the pool and pulled himself out, once again disdaining the steps, then faced her, to say with a frown, 'You're shivering. You should towel off.'

She shrugged and looked about her, hopelessly disorientated, for the tanning chair where she had laid her things.

'Never mind,' he said. 'The whirlpool's got no one in it. Let's talk there. It'll warm you up.'

'The *whirlpool*?'

He cocked an eyebrow. 'Why? Is that inappropriate? Did you want to sit in your swimsuit and have a nice little drink at the outdoor bar? Or would you like us both to get dressed and go out somewhere and make a real production of it? I haven't finished my swim yet.'

'Sorry to be such a nuisance.'

He looked at her for a moment, as if about to make an equally cutting retort, but evidently changed his mind and only muttered, 'Let's go.'

She followed him up the steps and through the screen of landscaped shrubbery. He pressed a button to activate the underwater whirlpool jets and they both stepped into the hot pool.

It was almost funny—to be having a confrontational talk here in this setting of sybaritic luxury. She crouched on one shelving seat and he stationed himself opposite, the familiar maleness of his body concealed by the foaming bubbles of moving water. She knew that body so well, and somehow that made this distance between them even harder to bear.

'So?' he challenged after a moment. 'What is it that you want to say?'

'Oh, come on, Richard!' It was half angry, half pained. 'You can't just. . .cut me off like this without any kind of explanation and without giving us any chance to work it out. That's unfair. . .wrong.'

She felt her emotion rising and fought to keep some control. She did not want to play the part of the scorned mistress, even though that was exactly how she was feeling, and it was absolutely horrible. She repeated stonily, 'You *can't*!'

'But that's where you're wrong, Nic,' he came in silkily at once. 'That's exactly what I *can* do. That's the beauty of our kind of arrangement. No commitment, remember? No strings attached? Which means that when either party wishes to terminate the contract for whatever reason—and I now wish to exercise that option—it can be done like that!' He snapped his fingers dismissively. 'Without all the endless earnest talking, negotiating, compromise, forgiveness and hard-slogging faith that makes most relationships so. . .so. . .' For once his fluency seemed to desert him.

'Such a nuisance?' she suggested coolly. 'So tedious?'

'Thank you. Yes. You see, you do understand the rules. You were a consenting party to them from the beginning so please don't try to change them to suit yourself at this late stage, Nic.'

'Stop *calling* me that!'

'I thought you liked it.'

'I *did* when it meant—Never mind!' She struggled once again for control. 'OK,' she had to concede, 'I— I— You're right, aren't you?' It gave her the most desolate feeling in the world to have to admit it. 'That is what no commitment means.'

At the beginning that hadn't seemed like a problem. At the beginning, though, she'd had no intention. . .no *capacity*, perhaps. . .to fall in love. She summoned some desperate flippancy. 'Well, it was fun while it lasted.'

'Yes, it was, wasn't it?' he agreed in a hard, cynical voice. 'But all good things must come to an end.'

'Except that if it was *good*, *still* good, for you, then I don't—'

She broke off. Someone else had arrived to use the whirlpool. A man, to be exact, over-tanned and wearing a swimsuit that Nicole found repellently brief. He hesitated for a moment at the lip of the whirlpool, then evidently sized up the situation and interpreted the thick silence between Richard and Nicole to mean that they were strangers to each other.

He slipped into the water with a grin and came at once to sit beside her. 'Nice night.'

She couldn't disagree.

'I don't think I've seen you here before.'

'I don't generally use the whirlpool.'

'Then the whirlpool's been missing out.'

Richard rose and waded to the steps, his wet torso steaming and his limbs glistening. 'I'll leave you to it, I think,' he murmured, not looking at her.

'Oh, please don't—' Nicole began, but was resolutely cut off by a cynical drawl.

'You know what they say. Two's company. . .'

'Now, that is a man I could like,' the newcomer drawled, too, as he moved an inch closer to Nicole.

Having ousted, as he saw it, the rival male, he was

now embarking on the courtship ritual. Nicole was very thoroughly not interested. She waited a barely decent interval, steering her way impatiently through the man's succession of hackneyed lines, then excused herself, found her towels and fled for the women's locker-room. She managed by sheer force of will to avoid looking for Richard's sleek body, cutting through the pale blue water of the pool.

CHAPTER NINE

So IT was over, even more suddenly and unexpectedly than it had begun. The hole that it left in her life made Nicole almost envy anyone going through a very messy divorce.

In that situation, at least, she thought rebelliously, I'd have to fight for custody of the compact disc collection and cash my alimony cheques. There'd be something to do!

She wasn't serious, of course. Her brother Adam, five years her senior, had been divorced four years ago and she knew what ugly scars it could leave—which is why she should probably have done a far better job of congratulating Barb Zelinsky when she called on the phone later that night to announce, breathless and a little giggly, 'Gary and I are getting married, Nicole. Isn't that incredible?'

Not so incredible, really. Nicole knew Dr Hill well enough to be sure that Barb had a happy married life ahead of her this time around. Both in their early forties and each with a divorce in their past, Barb and Gary had both been fairly open about wanting to marry again. So it was not incredible but very wonderful and it was completely selfish of her to be so daunted when Barb said, 'It doesn't matter if you can't make other plans. We'll wait if we need to. . .'

It was immediately obvious that to ask her to wait would be just too mean-spirited.

'But, you see, it would be great if I *could* fly back pretty soon, find someone to take Astro and get the house on the market because September is a good time. Otherwise it gets too cold and there are very few buyers

148

until March. I can't afford to have a slow sale.'

'So you'd like me to. . .'

'Whatever suits you best,' Barbara assured her. 'Stay on for the full year, if you want to. You'd be able to find an apartment easily enough, if you wanted to do that, and if you were losing out financially obviously Gary and I would cover the difference. Or stay just until September or October and then come home.

'That's a good two or three months from now, and gives Dr Gilbert plenty of time to find someone new. Then you can take up your old job and I'll become a lady of leisure while Gary and I decide whether we'd be crazy to try for a baby at my age.'

'Yes, or, as you say, I could find an apartment,' Nicole said rather dazedly, then added, thinking aloud, 'Except that I'd have to furnish it. I've been using all your things, of course. . .'

'We thought you probably *would* decide to come home early,' Barb agreed complacently, as if it was settled. 'You will have had six months. The nicest six months, too, for weather. Now that I'm experiencing what they laughably call winter here in Sydney. . . You might have a bit of a struggle with central Ohio's grey winter skies. But, of course—as I've said—if you *want* to stay I won't renege. I can even wait until March to sell the house. . .except that I think we *are* going to try for a baby and if I was pregnant by then. . .'

'I'll have to think about it and let you know. I hope you don't mind if I take a few days to decide on my plans.'

'Of course not. Take all the time you need. Even a week or so, if you have to.'

Barb clearly considered that she was being very generous, and perhaps she was. When you were in love patience could be an impossible virtue.

'It's wonderful news, Barb.'

'Isn't it, though?'

The obvious thing to do was to tell everyone in the practice at once, since they all knew Barb, of course, and would want to send a card or a gift. And yet she procrastinated and didn't mention it at all, quieting her conscience with the fact that Barb hadn't actually *said* in so many words, hadn't *asked* her to tell people, so maybe she'd meant not to.

Rubbish!

Nicole had to face the fact that she was deliberately staying quiet on the subject when Darla asked her casually on Thursday afternoon if she'd heard from Barb lately.

To say, 'No, not lately,' was an out-and-out lie, but she said it anyway, then added, as a pitiful sop to her conscience, 'But I think she's very happy.'

What was the point of this secrecy? To avoid the hard fact about her own life, of course. That the only thing to do was to leave in September as Barb wanted—it did make sense—and therefore never see Richard Gilbert again.

She was aching with the loss of what they'd had. The loss of *him*, it seemed, because although they would still see each other every day that was more pain than pleasure now. She was far more physically aware of him now at the office than she had been during the months they'd been sleeping together. It had been so easy back then to simply feel a warm, replete sort of glow at the sight of his male body in those soft, sexy scrubs.

Now, she felt *hungry* when she saw him, painfully so, in a way that tightened her muscles and churned her stomach and had her close to tears several times each day. How could a man who was as distant and stiff towards her as a two-dimensional plywood cut-out still set her on fire like this?

Evidently, however, she didn't have the same effect on him.

'The Powell baby is still surviving,' he told her stiffly on Friday morning. 'I just spoke to Will Hartman. Didn't tell you before, I don't think. . .' He frowned, then went on, returning her troubled gaze with a hard stare, 'Jennifer Powell asked me if there were any women in this practice who'd recently delivered prematurely and might be willing to donate breast milk. There aren't, I don't think, but if you'd check and mention it to the other nurses there may be someone we haven't thought of.'

'Denise Bliss?' Nicole suggested at once, absurdly eager to find an answer for him.

But he shook his head. 'She changed to formula after a few days, I understand, because she was too discouraged by pumping. Anyway, she had her six-week post-partum check-up last week. Her milk would have matured and changed. No, it has to be someone more recent.'

'There's Mary-Ellen Meer. She only delivered two weeks ago, nine weeks early.'

'Was she breast-feeding? Now why didn't I think she'd be suitable? I somehow think. . .'

'I'll check her chart, and give her a call.'

'Yes, do,' he answered abruptly, without the smile he would have used only a week ago to punctuate the words.

It had been a very special smile—as wicked and sensual and satisfied as the face of the cat who had got the cream. The heat of that smile had seemed to stay, to hang in the air, again like a cat—Alice's Cheshire cat. Now, though, when he disappeared into his office there was only a chilly little void.

Shaking off its influence, Nicole glanced at her watch and found she had a moment or two before it was time to start running patients. Those moments loomed large these days—far *too* large, with the opportunity they gave her for her painful feelings about Richard to surge to the fore. She got out Mary-Ellen Meer's chart and

looked it up and it *did* say that the second-time mother
had breast-fed before and hoped to do so again.

But when she got her on the phone a little later, and
worded her unusual and slightly sensitive request as
carefully as she could, there were tears and anger.

'My God, I couldn't *possibly*! Do you have any *idea*
how hard this is? To even get enough milk for *my* baby,
let alone someone else's! And when I'm so *incredibly*
worried about Joline I think it's very insensitive of you
to even ask! I mean, you nurses, who've never been
pregnant yourselves, you just don't have a clue!'

Nicole reported this response—or an edited version,
anyway—to Richard, and felt attacked again when he
answered, 'That's right. That's why I didn't think of
her. I knew there was a reason. She's a—' He stopped,
and amended, 'Let's just say, not one of my best-liked
patients. Call Jennifer Powell, then, would you, and tell
her we haven't had any success so far? Here's the
number she gave me. It's a motel, I think.'

'This is unusual, isn't it?' Nicole ventured. If she
couldn't ignore his hostility during working hours how
would she carry on with her job? 'Riverbank Ob/Gyn
doesn't normally organise breast-milk donations.'

'You think it's a waste of our time?'

'Not at all. I—'

'Call it a professional courtesy, then,' he came in
coolly. 'Dr Powell is very determined that this baby
should survive, and it's such a tragic situation. I felt a
need to help.'

'You don't have to explain yourself to me, Richard,'
she told him, her voice high and hard. She was hurt that
even this sort of exchange couldn't take place without
friction.

He muttered in reply, 'Don't worry. I have no intention of explaining myself to you, on this or any other
issue.' She just had to turn away.

Later she found time to phone the motel where

Jennifer Powell was staying, but there was no answer after she was transferred to the room so she waited until Reception picked up again and left a rather confused message. By the end of the day, though, Jennifer Powell hadn't returned the call.

It was now the weekend.

How dreadfully it dragged! She had been kidding herself until now that she had a social life here, but she didn't really. There'd been several outings with Gretchen, but she was dating again now and becoming less interested in a night with the girls.

Darla, too, hadn't asked Nicole to a family event for a while. I haven't encouraged it. I've only had the Hogans over once. I've let them think I was doing fine and, of course I was, with Richard to fill my days and nights. I hadn't realised how much I built everything around the time we spent together. . .

On Saturday night she rang Barb and told her that she would be coming home in September.

'You're right,' she summarised brightly into the phone, hiding what she felt. 'I think I've had the best of the experience now. It's been wonderful, of course. . .'

And all of that was truer than Barb could know.

On Monday Richard was out of the office, attending a seminar at the Ohio State University Hospital so there was a slight shuffle of nursing staff and Nicole was put on phone duty, which she hadn't done before.

Many of the calls came from gynae patients who had questions about pre- or post-operative care, hormonal problems or other difficulties, but the rest were from pregnant patients and it was amazing how many anxieties could develop, the most concerned and informed women often the most prone to panic! Was it all right to use nail polish in the first trimester? Was it dangerous to touch the animals in the petting area at the zoo? Could labour be triggered by too much swimming?

The commitment to their unborn children's health which lay behind these questions was important, even when some of the questions themselves seemed a little far-fetched.

Then, in the middle of all this, at about a quarter past ten came something more serious. Nicole could tell straight away from the tight tone and quickened breathing before she even knew who it was at the other end of the line.

'It's Kathy Solway. Is that. . .?'

'Hi, yes, it's Nicole.' She was fully focused now. Kathy's preterm labour nearly ten weeks ago had responded well to full bed-rest at home, and there had been no further problems. Now she was nearly thirty-two weeks, but that was still far too early to deliver safely. 'What's up, Kathy?' she asked quickly, knowing that this time it wasn't going to be a question about nail polish or swimming.

'I'm having pains again. I was stupid! Mike's parents arrive tonight and I couldn't stand having them see the house in such a state. I was so stupid!'

'Don't worry about that, Kathy,' Nicole soothed. 'Tell me about the pains. Is it like before?'

'No. . .stronger,' came the resigned, shaky reply. 'Much stronger. Quite painful now, and the last three each came like clockwork after four minutes. If only I hadn't ignored that first one! I wasn't vacuuming or anything really dumb like that, just putting away some laundry, but I guess I bent down to a drawer and at first I thought it was just strain because I'm getting heavy now and I'm not used to being on my feet with that weight. . .'

'You'd better come in. Is Mike there with you?'

'No, he's at work, but I've called him. He should be here in a few minutes.'

'Come straight in as soon as he arrives.'

'To the office?'

'No, better make it Labor and Delivery, I think, Kathy. They'll want to admit you this time.'

'Oh, *no*!'

'That doesn't necessarily mean you're going to have a baby today!' Nicole urged. She could hear that Kathy was crying now. 'There are other things to try first. Medication, hospital bed-rest. . .'

But Kathy's description of the pain sounded ominous, and Nicole had to add another blow, too. 'Dr Gilbert's not in today.'

'Oh, he's not?'

'Dr Turabian's covering. Have you met him?'

'No.'

'He's very good.' Of course he was, or he wouldn't be in this practice, but he was a stranger to Kathy, which added just that little bit more tension.

After ending the call with more reassurance, Nicole phone Labor and Delivery to tell them that Kathy was coming in, then told Berj Turabian what was going on as well.

He nodded. 'I'll expect a call from Labor and Delivery fairly soon, then. We'll mag her if we can.' He used the casual shorthand for treatment with intravenous magnesium sulphate, which could often halt preterm labour successfully. He added, 'But you're probably right. Too far along now.'

It *was* too far along. Kathy Solway delivered her baby boy, Andrew, at twelve-fifteen that afternoon and he was rushed straight to the neonatal intensive care unit.

'So many things can go wrong, can't they?' Elaine Bridgman said to Nicole, pushing her wheelchair through to the lab from the billing office just as the news came through.

'Yes, but far more often everything goes right,' Nicole answered her firmly. 'You're not really worried, are you? Nothing's giving cause for concern?'

'Just edgy, I guess,' Elaine admitted. 'It's getting so

close. I'm thirty-eight weeks now, and Caitlin will soon be born.' She and Paul had decided on this name soon after hearing from Richard that the ultrasound had indicated a girl. 'But, anyway, I didn't come through in order to complain. Or not *just* in order to complain!' She laughed her pretty laugh, and wiped a curtain of long dark hair behind her ear. 'Can you decipher the signature on this letter or tell from the context who it could be? It's really giving me a headache!'

She held out a handwritten screed that was very voluble in protesting the unjust excess of a series of medical bills but entirely silent on any identifying details. As Elaine had said, the name scrawled at the bottom was very difficult to read.

'Maddon?' Nicole hazarded. 'Malley? Malden? Walden?'

'Ring any bells?'

'Not really, but I haven't been here long enough to know everyone. Now, she says she "didn't have any pathology", which seems unlikely for a start.'

'If only she'd enclosed the print-out, or at least put in the account number, we could just punch her up on the computer.'

'She talks about regional anaesthesia but, again, that applies to so many things.'

'Never mind.' Elaine sat back in her wheelchair and stretched her upper limbs weakly. Her fine cotton smock top was getting distinctly tight around the middle, in contrast to the thin, motionless legs below which were encased in stretchy black leggings. 'I'll just stick the letter in a query file and maybe she'll write again with more details next time the computer sends her a bill.'

She whooshed a big, pregnant sigh, looking hot and damp despite the very adequate and at times positively glacial air-conditioning of the Riverbank Ob/Gyn office suite. 'But I *hate* unresolved accounts.'

She gave another sigh. That top was *very* tight,

making her abdomen beneath look as hard and round as a basketball. No, make that a football—the elliptical kind—because now it was mounding up even higher.

'Uh, Elaine. . .' Nicole said, just as Elaine started to tremble and sweat and press her hands to her head.

'Something's happening, isn't it?' she managed to say shakily. 'My blood pressure's taking off.'

'You're in labour, Elaine. Dr Gilbert really picked a bad day to have a seminar.'

'I should call Paul, then. Oh, my head, it's getting worse by the minute. And I'm dripping all over! Should I wait until Paul gets here?'

Somehow Nicole doubted it, but she said, 'I'll check with Dr Turabian. Let's take a look at your blood pressure first.'

As they'd both suspected, it was far too high and Dr Turabian wouldn't let Elaine wait until her husband arrived. 'Take her across now,' he told Nicole. 'I'll phone ahead and tell them to prepare her for an epidural straight away.'

This form of anaesthesia wasn't necessary to numb pain in Elaine's case, of course, as she had no sensation below the sixth thoracic vertebra, but it would act as a block to the unmodulated nerve stimuli from lower in her spine which was causing her dysreflexia.

'We need to bring her blood pressure down as soon as possible,' Dr Turabian was saying, 'and *then* we'll worry about the baby!'

Elaine was feeling too bad to control her own wheel-chair now so Nicole pushed it, going as fast as she could while still staying on the side of safety. If Elaine's blood pressure was still rising. . . Dysreflexia could be life-threatening if the trigger was not quickly removed.

A nurse from Labor and Delivery, an anaesthesiologist and a nurse-anaesthetist were waiting when they arrived and Nicole could hand her patient over to their care, even if she couldn't hand over all her own concern.

After dozens of lunches together with the rest of the
staff in the large, open lunchroom at Riverbank Ob/Gyn,
Elaine was a friend now.

'You'll be fine,' she told the pregnant woman. 'This
time tomorrow we'll all be descending on you in our
lunch-hour and cooing over baby Caitlin through the
nursery window.'

But Elaine was in the grip of the anxiety which was
one of the symptoms of dysreflexia and couldn't respond
coherently. She was struggling against tears and having
difficulty answering the questions and carrying out the
instructions that the nurse and the anaesthesia staff were
directing at her. Paul was trying his best to help, but
the end result was only to confuse her more. Nicole
knew she had to leave in order for Elaine to focus.

As she made her way towards the lift, though, her
path was blocked by a high, wheeled bed with a woman
on it, well draped in sheeting, and it was only when the
way widened so she could pass that she recognised
Kathy Solway, who was on her way from Labor and
Delivery to her post-partum room.

'I hear you have a boy, Kathy,' she said.

'Yes.' The other woman nodded rather dazedly. 'I—
I can't believe it. They haven't let me see him. . . They
whisked him away. The birth was. . . I was just so frightened. Mike's gone to the NICU. They say he. . .
Andrew. . .is looking good, but. . .'

She was wheeled away by a rather impatient orderly
and Nicole knew Elaine would be busy now, transferring
to her bed and getting checked again, all the while thinking only of the health of her child.

I'll come down again at the end of the day, Nicole
decided. To see Elaine and Kathy. They both need
support.

Fortunately the afternoon was uneventful. The whole
office knew that Elaine was in labour but, apparently,
progress was slow. The epidural had quickly taken effect

and her blood pressure had returned to normal, but the combination of her disability, her status as a first-time mother and the effect of the epidural meant that dilatation was taking time.

'At least this means that Dr Gilbert will deliver her,' Darla Hogan said at four-thirty as everyone was preparing to leave.

'I'm sure she'd have done fine with Dr Turabian,' said Ellen Glover, who was very loyal to the practice partner who claimed most of her time.

'I was thinking of Dr Gilbert,' Darla clarified. 'I know he'd like to see her all the way through since he did so much to encourage her confidence that she could actually *do* this!'

'Did he?' Nicole murmured, unable to help showing her interest. 'I hadn't realised.'

'Oh, yes! Both Paul and Elaine were sceptical for a long time about trying for a child, but Dr Gilbert convinced them that it was possible *and* that she had the commitment to see it through.'

Commitment.

Nicole frowned. What a pity he could bring it out in others, but didn't have it himself. She felt the knife-twist of her pain and said quickly, to cover it, 'Is anyone else going down to see Elaine now?'

'I'd like to,' Darla answered, 'but I have to pick up the kids.'

'Same here,' said Ellen and Stephanie.

'And Brian's picking me up at five,' Gretchen came in. 'I won't be ready for him as it is.'

'She won't want a crowd, will she?' asked Sarah Turner, who ran patients for Dr Mason and had only been with the practice for two months.

'No, she won't,' Darla agreed. 'But I'm glad you're going, though, Nicole, because if she's still only two centimetres she has a long wait.'

Elaine was far more relaxed than she had been a few

hours earlier when Nicole was permitted into her room
ten minutes later. Paul was there and they were watching
television together, flipping the channels between very
lurid afternoon talk shows, in between chatting cheerfully about the contractions on the monitor and the slight
changes in the baby's heart rate, which remained within
the normal range.

It was definitely a high-tech birth. The epidural anaesthesia prohibited any movement, and Elaine was
attached to an IV line as well as the tubing for the
epidural which was taped to her back, but as she'd
expected this sort of experience all along she wasn't
disappointed.

'I'm loving it, actually,' she told Nicole. 'Paul and I
are giggling away. Look at this show! Today's topic is
"Bike Style Make-Overs". Do you like the combination
of the tattoos, the blow-waved hair and the satin vest
on this guy? And, really, I'm in no pain and the baby's
just patiently waiting for her time to come out. I guess
at lunchtime I was panicking, but now. . .'

'That's great, Elaine.'

'And since things are slow Dr Gilbert will get to do
the honours after all. Hopefully not too much past his
bedtime.'

'Hopefully. . .' She hated the fact that it was so hard
to talk about him now, even in the easiest context, and
she desperately missed the little coil of secret delight
which had stirred within her until last weekend whenever she got the chance to mention his name.

She stayed five minutes more, then Nurse Susie Allan
came in again to do an internal check.

'Let's see how you're doing, shall we? How are those
contractions looking, Paul?'

He frowned. 'Actually, she hasn't had one for a while.
We've almost been forgetting to check.'

'Well, not to worry at this stage,' Susie said as she
put on fresh gloves.

Nicole ducked out and went in search of Kathy Solway's room. She found it easily enough but Kathy wasn't there, and Nicole guessed that she would be in the NICU with her baby boy.

Riverbank's Neonatal Intensive Care Unit was quite large, but after being buzzed in she found Kathy at once, standing beside her son's isolette with a yearning, hungry and still very dazed and helpless look on her face, while Andrew's nurse filled in his chart and checked on her other charge on this shift.

'The first forty-eight hours are the most critical,' Kathy said, after gliding mechanically over her greeting. She was obviously repeating what the doctors had told her. Then she added, like a mantra, 'He's one of the biggest and healthiest babies in the unit.'

'He is,' Nicole agreed.

Anyone who'd never seen a preemie before would have found it hard to recognise this, though. Baby Andrew still had the thin, red, almost transparent skin, the fine covering of colourless hair and the frog-like posture of a typical premature baby, but he was active and strong and breathing well with some assistance from a ventilator.

'I came down to see if there was anything you needed help with,' Nicole said, but Kathy was still too overwhelmed to have thought through her situation and her needs.

'I guess feeding is the next thing. They say he's not ready yet. I want to use my own milk. . .'

She lapsed into silence again, just watching her baby, but Nicole's mind was alive now with a new idea. Would Kathy be willing to donate milk for tiny Teresa Powell? Teresa wouldn't be in this part of the unit. It was divided into three sections, with the smallest and sickest babies at the far end while those who were 'just growing' and awaiting discharge were nearest the entry.

Andrew Solway fell in between these two groups and

was in the middle section, but he had a good chance of 'graduating' fairly soon to the healthiest group. Teresa Powell, of course, was not yet as fortunate.

Excusing herself quickly—although Kathy scarcely seemed to register the words—Nicole went along to the far end and saw that Jennifer Powell was there, sitting in a chair beside her niece's isolette with her head bent over a medical textbook.

'Hello, Dr Powell. We haven't actually met, but. . .'

The small, slim woman looked up and smiled uncertainly. She looked too young to be a doctor. 'Yes? You look familiar, but—'

'I'm Richard Gilbert's practice nurse. I left a message for you at your motel.'

'Oh, of course!' The shadowed eyes were suddenly eager and alive. 'I called your office late Friday afternoon but only got the answering service, and then I was caught up in everything here all weekend. I—It's been a difficult and confusing time.' She frowned, as if trying to collect her feelings. 'She's not ready for tube feeding yet, anyway. But have you found someone?'

'I don't know,' Nicole answered honestly. 'But there's a woman I'd like you to meet. . .'

She brought Dr Powell back to where Kathy still stood—she ought to be resting more, actually—and introduced the two women to each other, then took a back seat in the conversation as a tentative link was forged.

After a few minutes Jennifer Powell was too single-minded to spend any longer in working up to the subject. 'I'm looking for a breast-milk donor, Kathy. That's why Nicole wanted us to meet, and wanted you to hear my sister's story. I'm sorry. . . There's nothing in it for you, but Teresa *must* live, must thrive. . . Can you understand? Please think about whether you migh be able to do this for her!'

Kathy was silent for a long moment. 'I have no idea,'

she said. 'I'm willing. How could I not be? But this is so new—who knows if I'll succeed at pumping?'

'Would you like to see her?' Jennifer asked eagerly. 'She's so tiny.' She smiled. 'She makes your little guy look like a football player. But she's a fighter! If some sort of. . .financial compensation—'

'No,' said Kathy firmly.

'I'm serious.'

'So am I. For a start, I doubt anyone could tell us what breast-milk brings on the open market. . .'

For the first time there was shared laughter between all three women, as well as from NICU nurse, Judy Lawrence.

'As for Teresa,' Kathy went on, 'I'd love to see her.'

And that was all it took to convince Kathy that she could make the extra commitment needed to feed someone else's baby as well as her own. Nicole was able to step in and arrange tests to ensure that Kathy wasn't unknowingly carrying any diseases, as well as promising to organise storage jars and an electric pump. She then badly wanted to insist that Kathy go back to her room and lie down but, clearly, she wasn't yet ready to leave Andrew.

'When Mike comes,' she promised.

Nicole caught a glance from Judy Lawrence and read it correctly. I'll make sure she rests, it said. Nodding briefly, she touched Kathy on the arm. 'Hang in there!'

Then, after an equally brief goodbye to Jennifer Powell, she left the unit.

It was after six o'clock now, she realised with some surprise as she made her way back up to the Riverbank Ob/Gyn office suite to collect her things. Not that she had any pressing business for the rest of the day. She felt wiped out, too, fragmented by her concern for Elaine, Kathy and even Jennifer Powell with those haunting, shadowed eyes of hers—although they scarcely knew each other.

Would tiny Andrew Solway ride out these critical
first days of life without complications? Would baby
Teresa Powell even survive?

And why was she so concerned about Elaine's labour?
It was slowing down, and possibly Elaine didn't realise
that she might still be here, and still be pregnant, this
time tomorrow, but it was absurd to be so churned up
about it, absurd to feel this dark pool of foreboding.

I don't usually get over-involved like this. What's
wrong with me?

She knew, of course. It was Richard, and the loss of
what they'd had, eating away at the secure emotional
base which normally allowed her to keep any concern
over her patients—even when they were friends, like
Elaine—healthily in perspective.

She sighed as she unlocked the discreet staff door
of the Riverbank Ob/Gyn suite, which opened off the
carpeted corridor halfway between the elevator and the
main reception area. With any luck, the place would be
deserted now. She almost wanted to stay for a bit—tidy
her desk, prepare for tomorrow's patients, make some
tea—since home was so thoroughly untempting.

It would be hot, except for the window air-conditioner
in the bedroom, bereft of food unless she shopped for
groceries at the twenty-four-hour supermarket on the
way home, and very lonely now that Richard no longer
phoned or stayed. And with Barbara already making
plans to come over and organise painting and repairs to
prepare the place for selling, she was starting to feel like
just what she was—a temporary and no longer entirely
welcome guest.

She went into the staff lunch-room and heated a cup
of water in the microwave, jiggled a stale teabag in it
before it was really boiling and added the few drops of
milk that were left in a carton in the fridge, all without
registering one or two tiny sounds that came from the
far side of the office suite.

She tasted the tea and grimaced. Scarcely hot at all. Impatiently, she nuked it in the microwave again for a full minute so that the cup's handle was almost too hot to hold and the liquid itself was now sputtering.

Then, mug in hand, she went through the lab and along to her little alcove to sort things through a bit. Last month's on-call roster was still taped to the wall above the phone, for example. Taking a sip of the tasteless, scalding tea, she ripped off the sheet, crumpled it and tossed it into the waste-paper bin round the corner in the lab, then gasped with surprise as she turned back to see Richard emerge from his office.

Boiling tea slopped onto her hand and she felt the stinging shock of the burn travel up the nerves in her arm before the dropped mug even hit the floor.

If Richard had seen that she was burnt he certainly wasn't wasting time on sympathy, and his voice was a weary, irritable rasp as he demanded, 'What on earth are you still doing here? The job's not that demanding, is it? That you can't get it done in the hours you're paid for?'

It sounded like a rebuke, a criticism of her efficiency, and it wasn't just her hand that was burning as she knelt clumsily to try and sop up the tea with a single tissue before it sloshed into the dark green carpet.

One tissue was hopeless, of course, against a whole mug of tea. Richard made an impatient sound and lunged past her into room two to grab some towelling from a drawer, dealing with the spill in seconds.

She watched him in numb, frozen silence, ignoring the pain in her hand, and only answered his question after a long moment of complete befuddlement. 'I—I haven't been here all along. I'd only just come back from seeing Elaine and Kathy Solway on the maternity floor.'

'Making rounds?' he queried sarcastically. He'd been briefed by Dr Turabian on the status of both women, of course. Or possibly he'd called Labor and Delivery

himself for a report on the day. 'I wasn't aware that was
part of your brief.'

If there had been any humour intended it was buried
pretty deep, and she hated his tone, confronted by its
lack of familiarity after four months of believing that
she knew all his moods—four months of *loving* those
moods, too, especially the humour.

'I wasn't making rounds.' She struggled to defend
herself, completely incapable of finding her usual confident, incisive wit. 'Elaine's a friend. And as for Kathy,
today was a tough day for her. But she's going to donate
breast-milk for the Powell baby. Isn't that good?'

'It's great,' he answered automatically. 'Now, since
you've spilled your tea, why don't you go home?'

It was as merciless as a slap in the face, and she
reacted as if it had been one, flinching and feeling the
colour throb in her cheeks. Her hand was throbbing now,
too, and still burning.

There should be something to say—something utterly
clever and cutting, something that would *hurt* him—
only there wasn't. In the few seconds it took her to
accept this she simply stared at him, her chin raised so
that its trembling was painfully apparent as was her
heightened colour and her pain-moistened eyes.

He swore, then said her name. 'Nic!' That came out
like an oath as well. She would have turned and simply
walked away, but before she could do so, he reached out
with rough imperiousness and pulled her into his arms.

'Oh, *God*, Nic!' he muttered. 'I really think I hate
you now!'

CHAPTER TEN

THE words didn't penetrate. Or if they did they didn't matter, swamped as they were by Richard's kiss.

He was punishing Nicole. That was blatantly apparent at first. His arms held her like the tight metal coils of a spring and his mouth on hers was rough and careless. Very soon, though, this changed. Standing motionless against the onslaught of his ruthless touch, she gave a tiny whimper—daunted by the vital task of gathering her strength to fight him off when her body was already awakening to intoxication at the familiarity of his touch after its eight-day absence.

She had to do it, though. She *had* to fight him. She couldn't let him think that this, anything like this, was what she wanted. But it would be so *hard*! So she whimpered, her lips parted helplessly and something about the sound made his response change.

He wasn't rough now. Instead of imprisoning her, his arms softened into a caress that was hungry and insistent yet fluid, sensuous. He groaned, a deep vibration of sound that came from far inside him, and he drank the taste of her thirstily so that she had to gasp for breath as she turned her head back and forth, trying to escape that mouth—not because she hated his kiss but because, still, as always, she loved it.

She swayed back against the wall of the corridor and he followed the movement with a stride of his own so that she felt his thighs now, hard against her, supporting her and holding her in place. She was still trying to turn her head this way and that, back and forth, making it impossible for him to fully take her lips, but it didn't deter him—merely made him shift so that his mouth made a hot trail of need down her arched neck and she felt his dark hair slide against the sensitive skin of her throat, his head a familiar dark blur in the lower half of her vision.

How much she'd loved to have him cradled there over the past months! Her will crumbled under the onslaught of her senses and she let her head fall forward again. He immediately recaptured her, bringing his hands up now to cup her face and hold her there as she shamelessly returned every touch of his mouth while they both tasted her tears.

'Am I making you cry, Nic?' he growled. 'Am I? Yes, I can taste the salt of it. Good!'

'Yes, you *would* think like that, wouldn't you?' she stammered. 'It gives you pleasure to provoke emotion in other people, even though you're incapable of emotion yourself.'

'Incapable of emotion?' He took his mouth from hers just long enough to bark the words on an ugly laugh. 'Nic, I hate you like hell.' He rasped the words against her lips. 'I want you like heaven. That scarcely adds up to an incapacity for feeling, does it?'

'Oh, I think it does,' she answered harshly, feeling her anger growing and refuelling her strength and courage at last.

She turned her face from his once more and pressed the palm of her unburnt hand to his mouth to keep it away. He took the pads of soft flesh beneath her fingers between his teeth and bit—not hard enough to hurt, not gently enough to tease.

'Wanting isn't emotion,' she told him scathingly. She wanted him now, heaven help her, felt the nerve connection between her palm and her inner core like hot wires and could recognise the phenomenon for what it was. 'It's physiology. And as for hate, that's the absence of love—just as cold is the absence of heat. Oh, sure, when it's below freezing and the wind bites into your face cold *feels* like a force, but it's not. It's an absence, it's negativity and hate is the same. Absence and emptiness. So don't give me "emotion", Richard. In you, it doesn't seem to exist!'

He laughed. 'Isn't that a case of the pot calling the kettle black?'

'No! I—' She stopped. I love you? But she'd tell him *anything* rather than that at this moment. 'I despise you.'

'Which, according to your reasoning, isn't an emotion either,' he pointed out.

'Isn't it? *Is* it? I don't care, I really don't! Just let me go and leave me alone! You were the one who put an end to this. You were the one to make rules, talk about rules, enforce rules. Now you can damn well keep the wretched rules yourself!'

She hadn't expected him to respond, but he did. He dropped his hands suddenly—they had been pressed for the past half-minute against the wall on either side of her head—so that they hung lifelessly by his sides for a moment. Then he raised them again and seemed to seek her own hands quite blindly, taking them and lifting them level with his heart.

'All right,' he said through gritted teeth. 'I'm sorry, OK? I'm angry and I'm inflicting that on you. It's not helping either of us, is it?'

'N-no.' The evident sincerity of his regret undermined her totally. How could he possess such an impossible combination of honour and cruelty?

'I'll attempt a greater degree of control in the future,' he drawled.

'Please do!' Then she added impulsively, 'It will please you to hear, I'm sure, that it won't be for much longer. I haven't told anyone yet. Barb is marrying my boss, Dr Hill, in Sydney. She wants to sell her house in September and we've both decided it's best if I go back and take up my old job there instead of finishing this exchange. Now that I've adjusted to the change of plan you can feel free to start advertising for Barb's replacement as soon as you like.'

'September,' he said blankly. 'That's two months. Six weeks, in fact.'

'Not long.'

'Not long,' he echoed. 'How long have you known about this? Did you know about it when——?' He recast the sentence. 'Had Barb told you this ten days ago?'

'No, she hadn't,' Nicole answered, not seeing that it mattered in the slightest. 'She rang last Wednesday. I didn't mention it straight away because I needed time to think about what I wanted to do.'

'You mean there were other options?'

'Yes. She would have been content for me to see out the full year if I'd wanted to.'

'But you didn't.' His tone was wooden.

'I didn't,' she confirmed tightly, sick of this—sick of being with him when it only brought gut-twisting misery.

She pulled her hands from his then winced as the red, tender skin where the tea had spilled tautened and burned again painfully. He looked down and saw the angry colour there for the first time.

'That's not from the tea?'

'Yes, it——'

'You damned idiot! Why didn't you say something? Why did you try to mop up the spill? It wasn't important. You should have put that hand straight into cold water and kept it there for at least ten minutes.'

'I do know that,' she answered coldly. 'I'm a nurse. It's not a serious burn.'

'It's a painful scald. You've missed the chance now for the most effective first-aid you could have given it.' His dark eyes were accusing.

'Yes, I *know*,' she said. 'If you'll remember, our conversation got hot enough to overshadow the heat of this rather quickly.'

Still, now it was really hurting and she couldn't help wincing again as she flexed her hand.

'Let's soak it now and put something on it,' he suggested—*ordered*, really, as when she tried to dismiss the idea he completely ignored her, taking her elbow and pulling her along to the nearest sink around the corner in the lab.

The cold water, running over her hand, did feel good. Very good. Almost but not quite enough to distract her from the fact that his touch had now become utterly gentle. 'That's really starting to look nasty,' he murmured, separating her fingers gently and carefully as the cool water flowed over them. 'Are you up to date on your tetanus?'

'Yes,' she answered, mesmerised by the way his fingers were moving. Glistening with water, the fine dappling of hair on the third joint of each one was dark and streaming, and his nails were clean, thin crescents, which would be just long enough, as always, to scratch deliciously on her back or her hips or her thighs as they had done so often in recent months. . . Don't think of that now!

'Yes,' she repeated, 'I had a tetanus booster before I came over.'

'Good, because you've got blisters forming already and they'll get infected very easily if they break before any new skin forms beneath. Do you have any Silvadene cream?'

'No, I don't.'

'Pick some up on the way— Hang on! I'm not letting you drive home like this.'

'Don't be ridiculous. Of course I can drive!'

He was still exploring her fingers gently. 'You can't. The burn goes right down between your fingers, where your skin is incredibly fine.'

He'd kissed her in that tender spot between each finger many times, and he was thinking of it now. She could tell by the sudden rigidity in his body. But he didn't refer to the fact, of course. Instead, he continued, 'How can you possibly grip a steering-wheel safely? The pain alone will make it impossible and you won't have the control.'

'I'll phone for a taxi, then.' She shrugged. 'It's no great problem.'

It was far *less* of a problem, in fact, than his nearness—the light press of his arm against hers, the rhythmic ebb and flow of his breathing.

'Don't be an idiot, Nic,' he sighed. 'I'm going to drive you.'

'Oh, *are* you? You could do me the courtesy of *suggesting*, rather than ordering.'

'All right,' he said impatiently. 'I *suggest* you let me drive you home *and* that you let me stop off at Kroger's pharmacy department for some Silvadene.'

It seemed pointless to protest any further until she remembered. 'You're on call, aren't you? You took over from Dr T. at five.'

'I'll bring my pager, of course. And at the moment there's nothing going on. I was planning to go home, anyway. I need an evening to myself. The seminar today was fairly intense.'

'What about Elaine?'

'She's hours away from anything dramatic. In fact, the only thing I'll probably be doing for her this evening is starting her on pitocin. Her labour had slowed to a crawl when I phoned Labor and Delivery twenty minutes ago. Listen, why are we talking about this?'

'I don't know. Safe subject?' she suggested tartly.

'When in doubt I tend to prefer silence.'

'OK,' she answered in a light tone, which wasn't at all how she felt. 'Silence it is, then.'

And they were both true to the agreement, locking the office suite and walking down to the doctors' car park together through the humid early evening air without saying another word.

Their complete lack of communication gave her far too much opportunity to think of all the other times she had driven with him. That first day—when he had come to her rescue in the snow and there had been sparks between them from the first moment. Then, later on, driving to a restaurant or a movie or a park, when those initial sparks had flared into hot, sensuous coals and she'd felt free enough, sometimes, to rub her cheek against his shoulder as he drove. And, finally, the last time they had driven together—home from Hocking Hills eight days ago to stop at the supermarket, as they were doing now.

This time he was the one to go inside, returning a few minutes later to toss a small white paper bag into her lap.

'From what I could see of the burn, it'll do best without a dressing,' he said. 'Just wash it gently and put on the cream three or four times a day. If it's awkward overnight or at work you can put something on then. If you like, I can take a look at it tomorrow and Wednesday to see how it's doing.'

'That won't be necessary,' she told him. 'I'll be careful. And I'm not stupid.'

'I know you're not,' he muttered as he pulled up outside Barb's house.

'So, who's heard about Elaine? Nicole, have you? Cynthia? Gretchen?' Darla demanded as soon as she walked into the lab, a little late, the next morning. 'What time was our Caitlin born?'

'She hasn't been yet,' Cynthia answered. 'I looked in at seven on my way up.'

'Oh. . . Poor thing!' Darla groaned.

'Caitlin?'

'Elaine! Still, she's probably been able to sleep as she wasn't in any pain.'

'Getting a bit antsy when I saw her,' Cynthia said. 'Dr Gilbert's probably with her now.'

He returned a few minutes later to report. 'She doesn't want pitocin yet, and I'm not going to push as there's no sign of foetal distress or any other problem. But she's still only a bare four centimetres. If things don't pick up soon. . .'

Everybody made faces and noises of concern, but it was only Nicole's face that Richard saw and only her voice that he heard. He noticed that she had put a dressing on her left hand, sensibly choosing something dry and smooth that wouldn't adhere to the weeping skin of the burn. It would have been natural to ask about it but he didn't, irritated by the layers of truth and secrecy that surrounded their dealings with one another now.

What had she said about it to the others, for example? That he had caused it, as he felt he had? But if she hadn't mentioned his involvement then presumably he wouldn't know about it and it would be natural to—

Damn! He hated this! During their involvement together he had found the secrecy delicious, impossibly so at times as his body threatened to heat to boiling-point at the mere sight of her in the slim white uniform that accentuated her height and grace, her pale clear skin and her magnificent, living hair. Now, though. . .

'I'll be in my office, Nicole,' was all he said as he disappeared down the corridor, and he knew that behind him several of his staff would be exchanging speaking looks as only women could. He slammed his office door.

It was a tense day all round. Kathy Solway was discharged immediately after lunch, and phoned as soon as she got home in floods of post-partum tears, desperately eager to speak to him. He took the call in the privacy of his office, sensing that her need for his time was very real.

'I don't know what to do, Dr Gilbert,' she sobbed. 'I'm in such pain from the episiotomy.' As with many preemie deliveries, she had had a larger incision through the tissue of the perineum than would have been necessary if the baby had been at term to make the delivery as easy as possible for the fragile scalp tissue. 'All I want to do is to be with the baby but I must have overdone it yesterday. I'm so swollen and tender I can barely walk. My bladder doesn't feel right and I'm afraid I'm bleeding too much. I'm trying to pump milk but nothing's coming. . .'

He didn't have an answer because the only answers were time and rest, and he almost wished he'd given in to the temptation to invent a post-partum complication for her which would have bought her another precious day in hospital. But he knew her insurance company from previous experience and knew there would have been a follow-up call from some professionally suspicious number-cruncher, questioning his decision and looking for a reason not to cover the four-figure bill.

He said the only thing he could. 'Can Mike bring you in? Things looked fine this morning. Did they give you information sheets about breast-feeding and care of your episiotomy?'

'Yes,' came the reply, through more tears, 'but how can I learn all that from a few sheets of paper?'

'I know, it's rotten. Look, do come in when you can get here, and Nicole will spend as much time as it takes. She's a trained midwife, not just an Ob practice nurse, and she knows a lot about breast-feeding. We'll look at your stitches again, too, but I expect you're right and you've just been overdoing it.'

'How can I *not* overdo it!' She couldn't go on, and squeaked out on a sob, 'Sorry, Dr Gilbert.' Then she clumsily—judging by the noise in his ear—dropped the phone back into its cradle.

He sighed, buried his face in his hands for a moment and then straightened again as his pager went off. It was Labor and Delivery, of course, and when he phoned he heard Susie Allan's deceptively cheerful voice.

'I think you'd better come down, Dr Gilbert. The foetal heart rate's starting to slow perceptibly with each contraction. It was a sudden change, and with the last contraction it was quite marked.'

'Damn!' He'd seen Elaine again during the morning—still only just over four centimetres dilated—and this time he'd urged pitocin on her, but ironically her level of comfort and the presence of the internal foetal monitor with its constant electronic read-out was making her and Paul feel almost *too* secure after their nine months of worry. They were like sprinters, perhaps, who slowed without realising it just before they breasted the tape at the finish line. 'I'll be down straight away, Susie.'

He pulled open his office door and strode down the corridor, almost colliding with Nicole who had just ushered his second two o'clock appointment into room three. She tensed instantly and so did he which, as usual, was such a profound source of physical and mental turmoil to him that he simply barked, 'Elaine,' and dodged past her without any further explanation.

'Ready to deliver? Great, I'll alert the media,' Nicole answered, with a return of the spirit which had been high in this corridor for four months until its sudden disappearance nine days ago.

He wanted to give this change in her short shrift—children tended to behave badly when their treats were denied to them and, apparently, Nicole was still a child in this respect—but instead he was obsessed over it and probed it for another angle, a way to proceed that would be less. . .less damned *impossible* for him!

'No, *not* ready to deliver,' he told her, not mincing his words. 'Or rather, yes, by emergency C-section. The baby's in distress.'

'Oh, no!' She bit the sweet, full bottom lip that he ached to kiss and he turned away, with nothing more to say until he remembered. 'Kathy Solway's coming in. Give her a lot of time. She needs it.'

He was gone before Nicole even had time to nod at his last words. What a horrible day! she thought. Elaine's delivery going wrong at the last moment like this when they'd all relaxed about her pregnancy and almost started to celebrate baby Caitlin's birth already. And poor Kathy! Nicole didn't know exactly what was wrong, but it wasn't hard to guess at the possibilities.

She knocked on the doors of the two examining rooms that had waiting patients in them and told them that Dr Gilbert had gone to a delivery. One woman took it quite cheerfully and returned to the waiting room to devour the magazines, but the other had two energetic little boys to keep amused while she waited and Nicole heard her saying crossly, 'I *said* we'd go back to the part where the toys are. I didn't say you could play with all Dr Gilbert's equipment!'

The two-fifteen appointments would be on their way in already, but there was a chance that the two-thirties and two forty-fives could be rescheduled by phone.

'Did you manage it?' she asked Karen at the appointments desk a few minutes later.

'No luck with any of them,' she answered. 'I wonder what's happening with Elaine. . .'

Kathy Solway arrived before they had heard anything, having sent her husband, Mike, straight through to the NICU. In Dr Gilbert's absence, Nicole herself took a look at the painful swelling around Kathy's stitches.

'There's no infection,' she said. 'All you can do is stay in bed as much as possible. . .'

'Which I've been doing for the past ten weeks, anyway!'

'I know. It's hard. But it's the best you can do for Andrew. You did spend too much time on your feet yesterday because you wanted to be with him, but you must find a balance until you're physically in better shape. Take lots of shallow, lukewarm baths to keep the skin around the stitches soft and clean, and remember that you'll produce milk much more easily if you're rested and relaxed.'

'I hate this pump!'

So they took a look at that, too, and Nicole explained the importance of correct positioning and relaxation. Gently she held her palms against the sides of Kathy's breasts, judging the fullness through the practical cotton nursing bra and loose top. She told the other woman, 'Your milk hasn't even come in properly yet. Don't expect to get more than a little colostrum at this stage. You'll know that's what it is because it'll be quite yellow.'

'I feel like I was crazy to promise Dr Powell I'd donate milk for her niece. I even had the blood test to make sure I wasn't carrying anything. But when it's this much work to feed *one*. . .!'

'Don't take anything you're feeling today too seriously,' Nicole said. 'Just ride it out. If you can't produce enough milk for two babies Dr Powell will have to find another solution, that's all. Now, why don't you sit down in here quite quietly and try pumping. I'll come and check in a while and see how you've done.'

'Still no news on Elaine,' was the word when Nicole retreated gratefully into the lab for a few minutes. It seemed that was all anyone was talking about. Dr Mason kept appearing needlessly in the doorway of the lab, wearing a questioning look. Dr Smith, who was struggling round a hot, sunny golf course, had called twice from his mobile phone. Dr Kramer was trying to guess the timing.

'If they'd started prepping her for a C-section by the time Richard got down there,' she calculated, 'then general anaesthesia. . .closing the incision. . . We should have heard!'

'I've just told three patients that he's expected back any minute,' Nicole said.

'He usually calls, doesn't he, if there's any delay?' was Gretchen's comment.

It was nearly three already. Kathy called out from room three that she was getting some results now, and she was actually smiling and looked absurdly and very sweetly proud of the thin spread of yellowish fluid that covered the bottom of two sterile breast-milk storage jars. She brightened still further when Nicole offered to phone for a wheelchair to take her over to the NICU.

'Mike can get my doughnut cushion from the car and I'll really be riding in style!' So the worst was probably over in that area.

'But he's *got* to call soon about Elaine!' Nicole muttered a few minutes later as Mike arrived to wheel Kathy out.

Richard didn't call, though. Instead, he'd come in through the staff door and along to the lab before anyone realised he was back, and Nicole was the first to spot him.

'Well?' she prompted, and, as if it was a cue, almost the entire staff then materialised from offices or examining rooms to stare expectantly at him.

He looked horribly tired, Nicole suddenly saw, as if the day—or the week, perhaps—had drained him completely. He seemed at first to be uncertain where to start.

'I made a major mistake,' he began, and there were gasps all round. There was something about his expression, though, that Nicole recognised with dawning suspicion. 'But, fortunately,' he continued, 'the outlook is now good.'

'My God, Richard, what *happened*?' Dr Kramer breathed. 'Is Elaine in Recovery? Did you have to section her? Is the baby in the NICU?'

'Yes, it was a C-section,' he began very deliberately, his face completely sombre. Everyone was hanging on his words. 'Took a little longer than usual to repair the

incision because of previous scarring after her accident.
I dealt with a couple of minor adhesions and tidied up
a bit while I was in there. But, no, the baby's not in the
NICU. He's fine and he's probably with his mother
by now.'

'*He*?' Darla shrieked. 'But I thought it was a girl!
I've bought a dress already!'

At last Richard grinned. 'I told you I'd made a major
mistake. Admittedly, the baby's position when we were
doing the ultrasound ten weeks ago wasn't great, but I
could have sworn that what I'd seen on that screen
wasn't male equipment. Wrong! Fortunately Paul and
Elaine hadn't yet invested very heavily in little pink
dresses. . .'

'I'll have to return it—hope I've saved the receipt,'
Darla said. 'Oh, Dr Gilbert!'

'I expect there'll be some controversy in the name
department when Elaine's less groggy. Paul's talking
about calling the little bruiser after his paternal grandpa
whose name, I'm afraid, is Cyrus.'

The laughter that followed was as much from relief
as amusement, but Beth Kramer said threateningly,
'Richard, you gave us a horrible moment there!'

'Do you think I'd have said it that way if there'd been
a real problem?'

'I guess not,' Dr Kramer conceded. 'But when we
knew you'd gone down in response to an urgent call. . .'

'The baby was showing signs of distress and the amni-
otic fluid had a small amount of meconium staining by
the time we delivered him, but we got him suctioned
and cleaned before he breathed any of it in and his
Apgar score at five minutes was a perfect ten—which
is about what my reputation *used* to be for getting the
sex right on a sonogram.'

'It's not regarded as grounds for a malpractice suit,
Richard,' Beth Kramer soothed.

'And now, Nicole, how many patients do I have waiting?'

'A perfect ten,' she echoed. 'With two more due any minute. Karen couldn't get on to any of them by phone at home, and so they all turned up and decided to wait.'

'Let's get on with it, then,' he said.

It was five o'clock by the time they surfaced and, handicapped a little by her still-painful left hand, Nicole took slightly longer than usual to clean up, which meant that she was leaving just as Richard emerged from his office to head back to the maternity floor for a quick evening round, checking two of Dr Smith's patients who had delivered in the early hours of the morning.

They eyed each other, judging the distance to the door. Nicole was going to get there first. He stepped back to allow her to increase her lead, and she couldn't help glaring angrily at him. What a wilful waste all this hostility and distance was, it seemed to her, of something they'd had that had been precious.

'Got a date?' she asked with sweet, deliberate bitchiness, tossing the words back over her shoulder.

'No. Have you?'

And she couldn't resist retorting as they walked towards the elevator, 'Yes, with the wonderful man we met in the whirlpool at Mill Run last week. He's going to show me his hub-cap collection, then let me supply him with hot dogs and beer at regular intervals while he falls asleep in front of sport on TV.' It was stupid to talk like this. The words cut her more than they could possibly be hurting him.

'I'm glad you've found a soul-mate,' he said.

'I was joking, Richard,' she answered, weary of the pointless game.

'So was I.' They entered the elevator together. 'But we're not very funny, are we?'

'Not in the least. See you tomorrow.'

'You, too.'

They parted, and she made a very necessary stop at Kroger's supermarket on her way home, restocking with enough supplies to give herself two very large bags to carry up Barb's steps when she reached home.

And there was Richard on the porch swing, rocking it absently an inch or two from side to side. She heard the squeak of it before she saw him, then almost dropped her heavy bags as he rose to his feet.

'Took your time,' he said.

'You can see why.' She put the bags down to unlock and open the front door. Why on earth had he come? He was attempting to help her with the bags now, but she fended him off. 'Don't bother.'

'No bother.'

She turned to him, lifting her chin and standing in the doorway to block his entrance—determined to show him at least *some* pride and spirit. 'There's no point to this, is there? To you coming here? I certainly don't have anything more to say. It's over—we've agreed on that—and I'm left wondering why on earth we wasted our time on it in the first—'

But she gasped and couldn't finish as he took her arms in a painful grip, his dark eyes blazing and his jaw clenched. 'It's *not* over! Not for me!' A short, searing kiss burned across her lips. 'I'm tempted to insist that we're doing it on *my* terms from now on, not yours, but since I know that you'd run, literally, or fly—perhaps, in a nice jumbo jet—ten thousand miles to escape me if I made such an ultimatum I'll take it on *your* terms.'

He had frightened her, briefly, with the blatant, deliberate use of his strength. Her heart was thudding and her breathing was high and shallow but her fear had already ebbed, to be replaced by an onslaught of desire so fierce that it made her tremble. His maleness was swamping her, overwhelming her like a torrent and making her legs go weak.

He could feel it, too, and he was using it, wanting to

see this response in her. There was triumph as well as anger and will blazing in his face now.

'Yes,' he growled. 'The original groundwork's still there, isn't it? You still want *that* from me. Ten days ago I thought I wasn't prepared to take just that—that I'd rather have nothing than accept less than *half* of what I really wanted—but I've found I was wrong. So this is my capitulation, Nicole. If I can't have your love, if you haven't got that in you—total, all-encompassing, lifelong love—then I'll have what *is* strong in you— your passion and your sensual fire.'

His fingers raked across her breasts, then down to her hips and he pulled her against him so she could feel the blatant urgency of his arousal. She moaned and fell against him, her mouth fully open to take his kiss so deeply she could hardly breathe, and what he was actually saying almost didn't penetrate.

Almost didn't. 'Love?' she stammered dazedly. 'Why are you suddenly talking about *love*, as if—'

'Because *I love you*, and I won't pretend any more that I don't. I won't follow your glib, shallow little philosophy of "no commitment" any longer because I despise it and I despise what it's done to my relationship with you. I should have cut that little idea out of the very heart of our dealings with each other right at the beginning, instead of thinking I could play along with your rules until you realised you wanted to throw them out.'

'*My* rules?' she said blankly. 'You were the one who kept harping on about rules—until I was totally sick of the subject. *You* were the one who. . .who broke it off, who wouldn't even *talk*, because according to the rules of "no strings attached" relationships I had no right to expect the slightest explanation. And now you're saying. . . How *dare* you say you love me? As if you've known it all along and have just been *pretending*—'

'Because I do, Nic,' he answered, suddenly very calm.

'And I have been. Not pretending, perhaps, but holding myself back. And I can't do it any more. Here.' He heaped his hands together as if to make a small package. 'Here is my heart. Take it and do what you want with it. It's yours, OK? I'm giving you the Hope diamond, and I don't care if all you've got to give back is a quarter-carat cubic zirconium. I'll take it. Make you happy?'

He grinned lopsidedly, but there was a bleakness deep in his eyes and her dawning understanding of what was going on here suddenly encompassed the fact that he didn't *know*. Didn't know that if his love was the Hope diamond then hers was at least the Star of India.

It was too much. She felt tears spring into her eyes, sniffed twice, stared down and then felt his arms enclose her softly. 'Nic? What is it?'

His lips brushed her hair, then came to seek her mouth as he drew her gently inside the house at last and closed the door behind them, leaving her shopping bags in solitary state on the wooden porch. She nuzzled him, wanting much more of this but needing to talk first. Pushing his mouth firmly away with her fingers, she began to speak.

Haltingly, and without brushing it off or using the lightness of humour, she told him in careful detail the full truth about Colin, to finish finally, 'So when I started to love you. . .' she looked up to meet the triumphant flare of his gaze '. . .it took me a long time to know it, Richard.'

'When *did* you, then?'

'Not until ten days ago when I found out I wasn't pregnant, and realised how much I'd wanted to be.'

'Wanted to be?' His eyes had narrowed and his arms were stiff and tight around her now. 'You were appalled at the idea!'

'Because I thought *you* would be. Oh, those hours of suspecting the symptoms! I was so terrified of losing what we had, although I still didn't understand what it was—that it was love. I was sure you'd want to have nothing more to do with me or a baby. I mean, getting pregnant—the ultimate breaking of the rules, wasn't it?'

'And I was desperately hoping you *would* be pregnant, and that you'd realise then that you felt the same as I did.'

'Why did you hide it for so long?' she asked.

'You hadn't told me about Colin, but it wasn't hard to tell that you'd been frightened off. Once bitten, twice shy. You were like a spirited colt who'd had a bad master. I could see all the promise in you—the life and the beauty. I loved those qualities almost from the beginning, from those first moments in the snow, but I could see how skittish and mistrusting you were, too. If I'd started talking about marriage then. . .'

'Are you talking about marriage now?'

'Just try suggesting any other option and see how far you get!'

'Well, there's always—' she began teasingly.

'There's marriage,' he interrupted firmly. 'With kids, too, thanks! I'd like to respectfully request your help in getting rid of the professional liability of my childless-ness as soon as possible.'

She frowned. 'I'd never thought a lot about being pregnant myself. . .'

'You hadn't?'

'Not until that day at Hocking Hills. And then, when I wasn't busy being horrified, it felt. . .'

'Yes?'

'So *right*, Richard. So completely right to think of our joining together to make a baby and then me carrying it for nine months.' She looked at him. 'So, yes, I'd be very happy to marry you *and* help you get rid of that liability, my love.'

She tasted the word and itched to repeat it, but he wasn't giving her the chance. Nothing could have escaped from her lips against the onslaught of his kiss, and soon they both needed much more than that— needed to rediscover everything they'd shared physically with each other over the past few months, everything they'd both yearned for so desperately over the past ten days.

Her bed wasn't made. She groaned as they tumbled through the doorway into the air-conditioned cool of the bedroom and she rediscovered the state of chaos she'd left the cream and white polka-dot sheets in this morning.

'I can see I'm going to have to retain the services of my housekeeper after the wedding,' he murmured.

'Does she work on weekends?'

'No.'

'Good! Do retain her, then!'

'But why not on weekends?'

'Because I hope we'll frequently be sleeping late. As for the messy bed. . . Sorry!'

'I love it. It gives me ideas.'

'I think you already have quite enough ideas in that department, Richard.'

'Good heavens, no! You haven't heard half of my ideas yet.'

'Oh, really? Such as. . .?'

'Such as—No!' he interrupted himself firmly. 'Far better to show than tell, I think. . .'

And so he did show her, in great detail and at great length, so that it was really quite exhausting and they both slept afterwards. . .until she rolled him onto his side to cuddle him and whisper, 'Stop snoring! Let's get up and eat. I want to call Barb and tell her she can come and sell the house as soon as she likes.'

'And tell your Dr Hill he'll be needing a new nurse. This is really very convenient, isn't it?'

'Very. Shall we have the wedding soon?'

'I'll check my roster for the coming week, if you like.'

'Hmm. Let's give my family a chance to make it.'

'Let's give them a choice. Maybe they'd rather wait and come over for the birth.'

'Maybe they would,' she agreed, winding an arm around him and wondering if perhaps dinner and calling Barb could wait a bit longer after all.

Possibly Richard was of the same idea. He was certainly rather silent, and she felt a coil of very delicious satisfaction at the thought that his response to her body could occupy him so thoroughly.

'May I ask you something, Nic?'

'Of course,' she answered, full of smug, creamy anticipation. Could he make love to her again? The answer was yes!

'I don't *really* snore...do I?' he growled. 'You're teasing me when you say that, right?'

'Richard, is *that* what you were thinking about just now?' she responded on an indignant squeak.

'Er, yes, it is, actually...'

So much for her rosy fantasy about his sensuous preoccupation with her! Did he really snore, indeed! Severe punishment was clearly in order. Very severe.

So she smiled sweetly and said with kind and very deliberate condescension, '*Do* you snore? *Am* I teasing? Well, now, I'm afraid you'll never really know, will you, my darling?'

**Will Hartman has his own wonderfully
touching story
Look out next month for
MIRACLE BABY**

MILLS & BOON®

Medical Romance™

COMING NEXT MONTH

HOME-COMING
by Margaret Barker

Everything changes, and when Alice returned to Ceres she had to admit that Nick's change from boy to man was definitely a change for the better.

MIRACLE BABY
by Lilian Darcy

Jenny prayed for a miracle to save baby Teresa's life and then William Hartman arrived, the answer to her prayers.

ALL THE CARE IN THE WORLD
by Sharon Kendrick

Nancy's intentions were good—she would keep her relationship with Callum on a strictly professional basis—but they were proving difficult to keep.

DOUBLE TROUBLE
by Margaret O'Neill

Looking after twins single-handedly was enough to put anyone's life on hold, but James was determined that the time had come for Kate to live again.

Available from WH Smith, John Menzies,
Martins and Tesco

PARTY TIME!

How would you like to win a year's supply of Mills & Boon® Books? Well, you can and they're FREE! Simply complete the competition below and send it to us by 31st August 1998. The first five correct entries picked after the closing date will each win a year's subscription to the Mills & Boon series of their choice. What could be easier?

BALLOONS	BUFFET	ENTERTAIN
STREAMER	DANCING	INVITE
DRINKS	CELEBRATE	FANCY DRESS
MUSIC	PARTIES	HANGOVER

S	O	E	T	A	R	B	E	L	E	C
T	E	F	M	U	S	I	C	D	D	H
S	U	I	V	Z	T	E	Y	R	A	A
N	E	N	T	E	R	T	A	I	N	N
O	B	V	E	R	E	H	K	N	C	G
O	J	I	F	O	A	L	R	K	I	O
L	M	T	F	V	M	P	U	S	N	V
L	P	E	U	Q	E	N	Z	S	G	E
A	W	G	B	X	R	C	T	B	Y	R
B	F	A	N	C	Y	D	R	E	S	S

C8B

Please turn over for details of how to enter...

HOW TO ENTER

Can you find our twelve party words? They're all hidden somewhere in the grid. They can be read backwards, forwards, up, down or diagonally. As you find each word in the grid put a line through it. When you have completed your wordsearch, don't forget to fill in the coupon below, pop this page into an envelope and post it today—you don't even need a stamp!

Mills & Boon Party Time! Competition
FREEPOST CN81, Croydon, Surrey, CR9 3WZ
EIRE readers send competition to PO Box 4546, Dublin 24.

Please tick the series you would like to receive if you are one of the lucky winners

Presents™ ❏ Enchanted™ ❏ Medical Romance™ ❏
Historical Romance™ ❏ Temptation® ❏

Are you a Reader Service™ Subscriber?   Yes ❏   No ❏

Mrs/Ms/Miss/Mr ....Intials ....
(BLOCK CAPITALS PLEASE)

Surname..

Address ....

....

....Postcode............................

(I am over 18 years of age)   C8B

One application per household. Competition open to residents of the UK and Ireland only. You may be mailed with offers from other reputable companies as a result of this application. If you would prefer not to receive such offers, please tick box. ❏

Closing date for entries is 31st August 1998.

Mills & Boon® is a registered trademark of Harlequin Mills & Boon Limited.

Karen Young

SUGAR BABY

She would do anything to protect her child

Little Danny Woodson's life is threatened when
he witnesses a murder—and only his estranged
uncle can protect him.

"Karen Young is a spellbinding storyteller."

—Publishers Weekly

1-55166-366-X
AVAILABLE NOW IN PAPERBACK

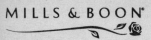

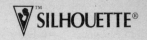

SPECIAL OFFER £5 OFF

FLYING FLOWERS

Beautiful fresh flowers, sent by 1st class post to any UK and Eire address.

We have teamed up with Flying Flowers, the UK's premier 'flowers by post' company, to offer you £5 off a choice of their two most popular bouquets the 18 mix (CAS) of 10 multihead and 8 luxury bloom Carnations and the 25 mix (CFG) of 15 luxury bloom Carnations, 10 Freesias and Gypsophila.

All bouquets contain fresh flowers 'in bud', added greenery, bouquet wrap, flower food, care instructions, and personal message card. They are boxed, gift wrapped and sent by 1st class post.

To redeem £5 off a Flying Flowers bouquet, simply complete the application form below and send it with your cheque or postal order to; **HMB Flying Flowers Offer, The Jersey Flower Centre, Jersey JE1 5FF.**

ORDER FORM (Block capitals please) Valid for delivery anytime until 30th November 1998 MAB/0198/A

Title ....Initials ....Surname ....

Address...

....

....Postcode ....

Signature..Are you a Reader Service Subscriber **YES/NO**

Bouquet(s)**18 CAS** (Usual Price £14.99) **£9.99** ☐　**25 CFG** (Usual Price £19.99) **£14.99** ☐

I enclose a cheque/postal order payable to Flying Flowers for £.................................or payment by

VISA/MASTERCARD ☐☐☐☐☐☐☐☐☐☐☐☐☐☐☐☐ Expiry Date............./.............../...........

PLEASE SEND MY BOUQUET TO ARRIVE BY........./.........../.........

TO Title ....Initials ....Surname ....

Address...

....

....Postcode ....

Message (Max 10 Words) ....

Please allow a minimum of four working days between receipt of order and 'required by date' for delivery.

You may be mailed with offers from other reputable companies as a result of this application.
Please tick box if you would prefer not to receive such offers. ☐

Terms and Conditions Although dispatched by 1st class post to arrive by the required date the exact day of delivery cannot be guaranteed. Valid for delivery anytime until 30th November 1998. Maximum of 5 redemptions per household, photocopies of the voucher will be accepted.